British Library Women Writers

Stories for Mothers & Daughters

First published in 2025

This anthology published in 2025 by
The British Library
96 Euston Road
London NW1 2DB
bl.uk

Volume copyright © 2025 The British Library Board

Every effort has been made to trace copyright holders and to obtain their permission for the use of copyright material. The publisher apologises for any errors or omissions and would be pleased to be notified of any corrections to be incorporated in reprints and future editions.

Cataloguing in Publication Data
A catalogue record for this publication is available from the British Library

ISBN 978 0 7123 5537 7
e-ISBN 978 0 7123 6868 1

Series editor Alison Moss
Story selection Molly Thatcher, Simon Thomas, Lucy Evans

Text design and typesetting by JCS Publishing Services Ltd
Printed and bound by CPI Group (UK), Croydon, CR0 4YY

Contents

Introduction	v
Publisher's Note	xv
Week-End *by Richmal Crompton*	1
Maternal Devotion *by Sylvia Townsend Warner*	11
The Value of Being Seen *by Inez Holden*	19
Psalms *by Jeanette Winterson*	29
The End of the Fairy Tale *by Maude Egerton King*	37
The Pictures *by Janet Frame*	49
The Silver Cloak *by Winifred Holtby*	55
History Again Repeats Itself *by E. M. Delafield*	65
Mothers and Daughters *by Frances Gray Patton*	83
The Shadow of Kindness *by Maeve Brennan*	103
Rose-Coloured Teacups *by A. S. Byatt*	119
Love is Not a Pie *by Amy Bloom*	127
The Battle-Field *by Phyllis Bottome*	147
I Stand Here Ironing *by Tillie Olsen*	169
The Stepmother *by Mary Arden*	179
My Mother *by Jamaica Kincaid*	199
Copyright Notices	207

Introduction

This collection of stories embraces the mother-daughter relationship in all its complexity, told through the masterful work of women writers. Taken from nearly every decade of the twentieth century, the familiar echoes and refrains of mother-daughter relationships carry across the pages and through the years. A series of ever-more-modern daughters chafe against the stasis of their mothers' eras and embody the evolving role of women in society. Mothers perpetually worry over imparting experience, balancing their individual hopes and dreams with societal expectations of motherhood, and grapple with the new freedoms their daughters represent. Alongside these recognisable concerns are figures who could only exist at certain historical moments: an Edwardian mother whose daughter is raised by servants, a debutante daughter of the Bright Young Things era, and a single mother struggling with poverty during the Second World War. Overwhelmingly though, these stories speak to the complex love and tenderness that exist between mothers and daughters without cliché or sentimentality. *Stories for Mothers and Daughters* is a collection about fallible origins and unstable futures, carried between generations of women into our modern age.

We begin with a mother preparing to welcome home her three

raucous daughters and their friend, down from London for the weekend. From the moment the girls arrive, 'Week-End' (1931) by Richmal Crompton becomes a cacophony of exclamations and shrieks that fill the quiet country cottage and remind the mother of the girls' late father. While the racing energy and chaotic chatter of the daughters is infectious, it is the bittersweet shyness of the mother and her desire for solitude that lends the story its heart.

Crompton (1890–1969) often portrayed complex, uneven relationships in her fifty or so novels and short-story collections for adults, but is best-remembered for the well-meaning, irrepressible William Brown in the *Just William* stories.

While Crompton's mother welcomes the sudden peace of her daughters' departure as if 'her lover had come back to her,' Cordelia, in Sylvia Townsend Warner's story 'Maternal Devotion' (1947), has no problem using her eccentric, monologuing mother to dispose of unwanted lovers. As Warner tells us with a characteristically feline simile:

> As kittens bring in the mice that are too much for them to be finished off by the cat, Cordelia Finch had a habit of depositing any inconvenient suitors with her mother and leaving the rest to nature.

We don't see much interaction between Cordelia and her mother, but we learn everything we need to know about the particular maternal devotion of the title. Sylvia Townsend Warner (1893–1978) also explored female eccentricity and unconventional living in her first novel, *Lolly Willowes*, about a spinster who runs away from her family to become a witch. Though British and living in Dorset for much of her life, 'Maternal Devotion' was published in *The New Yorker*, like much of Warner's short fiction.

The power of convention – particularly expectations of courtship and marriage – to define mother-daughter relationships is the focus of Inez Holden's story 'The Value of Being Seen' (1945). 'The important thing is to be seen,' Mrs Ascot advises her daughter, Daphne, when she reluctantly begins the debutante circuit of endless dances and husband-hunting. But motherly advice can be difficult to follow and as Daphne finds herself growing increasingly invisible to society and her mother alike.

Inez Holden (1903–1974) published several novels and short-story collections and was well connected with various luminaries of the mid-century: she was a close friend of George Orwell, sat for artist Augustus John, inspired a character in a Stevie Smith novel and briefly lived in a flat above H. G. Wells's garage.

Maternal advice comes in the form of a pet in Jeanette Winterson's darkly funny story 'Psalms' (1998). But while many daughters receive pets to learn responsibility, Psalms was 'bought for me and named for me by my mother in an effort to remind me continually to praise the Lord.' Winterson uses Psalms to epitomise the chafing relationship between a devoutly, even excessively, religious mother and her spirited daughter. It's a specific variety of mother-daughter relationship that Winterson (b.1959) explored at greater length in her semi-autobiographical debut novel, *Oranges Are Not the Only Fruit* (1985), and recurs throughout her fiction. Most recently, she published a collection of ghost stories, *Night Side of the River* (2023).

The earliest story in the collection, 'The End of the Fairy Tale' (1911) by Maud Egerton King inverts the expectation of a very modern daughter with a very modern mother – 'fashionable in everything save her motherhood.' If Winterson's mother is steadfast in her Christian duty to her daughter, King's childlike, high-society mother is from the era of alternating maternal neglect and frivolous abundance. Agreeing to tell her daughter, Aurelia, a fairy-tale before bed she finds herself questioning her own moral integrity. The action of the story is mainly contained to the upstairs nursery, while the adult world and the implications of an unexpected gentleman visitor linger downstairs.

As well as working as an author, Maud Egerton King (1867–1927) was passionate about weaving and social work, teaching local women to weave as an alternative to domestic service.

Hints of a complicated adult world also flicker around the edges of simple pleasures in 'The Pictures' (1951) by Janet Frame, one of the shortest and gentlest stories in the collection. Rather than a moment of change or crisis, 'The Pictures' shows the ordinary, everyday experience of an unnamed woman and her young daughter going to the cinema. Frame gives small hints about their life, without revealing too much – but 'The Pictures' still offers an oasis of joyful connection between mother and daughter.

> The little girl laughed. She clapped her hands and giggled and the woman laughed with her. They were the happiest people in the world.

Janet Frame (1924–2004) is one of New Zealand's most celebrated authors. She was famously scheduled for a lobotomy that was cancelled when her debut short-story collection – *The Lagoon and Other Stories*, in which 'The Pictures' appears – was unexpectedly awarded a national literary prize, days before the procedure was meant to take place. Several of Frame's stories and novels are influenced by her experiences of mental illness and psychiatric hospitalisation.

Winifred Holtby's posthumously collected 'The Silver Cloak' (1937) has a dramatic impact on wearer and observer. Dressmaker Annie was married at eighteen and very young when she had her daughter, Katie, and:

> She felt sorry for mothers who were so much older than their daughters that they couldn't share all the jolly things like clothes and parties and dancing.

But when gifted the titular silver cloak, Annie's appearance unsettles this close relationship. Holtby (1898–1935) sets the story in East Riding, a real county of Yorkshire, though Holtby is more famous for the fictional South Riding, being the title of her best-known, posthumously published novel. Holtby was an ardent campaigner for causes including feminism, socialism and pacifism. She was only 37 when she died of a kidney disease.

Much of Holtby's journalism appeared in the feminist journal *Time and Tide*, where the next author in the collection also frequently appeared. E. M. Delafield (1890–1943) is most remembered for the *Diary of a Provincial Lady* series, but had a prolific output of stories, novels, plays and non-fiction. 'History Again Repeats Itself', from the collection *Women Are Like That* (1929), features an energetically modern 19-year-old, Theodosia, and her mother 'who could easily have been a sentimentalist, but for Theodosia's bright, kind repressions of her'.

Theodosia adopts an artless air of superiority to her mother's generation – from the role of women to relationships between the sexes. A young woman of the 1920s, she is given to psychoanalysis, 'an advocate of Communism, Legalized Polygamy, Birth-Control', and considers herself above the silly flirtations of 'making love'. But as the story unfolds, Theodosia realises that her modernness may not be as unassailable as she believes, and some truths may be universal. Delafield often returned to the theme of self-deception, including in her novel *Tension* (1920), re-published in the British Library Women Writers series.

Skipping forward a generation, Frances Gray Patton's 'Mothers and Daughters' (1952), is another story of familial tension. 'Laura's always lovely to everyone but me' Emily tells her sister, Belle, who responds 'She's going through a phase.' They are both expressions that echo through the seventy-plus years since Patton's story was published, capturing something timeless about the challenges of parenting a teenage daughter. Prompted to remember themselves at Laura's age, specific generational trappings fall away, instead revealing the perpetual bravado and romantic idealism of youth. By the end of the story, Emily and Belle have transitioned in their minds from mothers to daughters. Frances Gray Patton (1906–2000) was an American short-story writer and novelist, with her greatest success being the bestselling novel *Good Morning, Miss Dove* (1954), adapted into a film starring Jennifer Jones.

As with Emily in 'Mothers and Daughters', we see Mrs Bagot as both mother and daughter in Maeve Brennan's 'The Shadow of Kindness' (1965). With her children staying with relatives for a month, Mrs Bagot feels bereft.

> She didn't know what to do with herself when they were away. Without them the house had neither substance nor meaning. [...] It was not right to let yourself get so lost in your children that you could find no trace of yourself when they were gone.

The solace she finds is unexpected but demonstrates the comfort that can be passed on through generations of mothers and daughters, especially in the loneliest moments. Most of Maeve Brennan's (1917–1993) short stories were published in *The New Yorker*, where Brennan also worked as a social diarist. She was born in Ireland but moved to the US as a teenager.

If the spirit of generational legacy is an uncomplicated blessing for Mrs Bagot, Veronica, in A. S. Byatt's 'Rose-Coloured Teacups' (1987), sees it as something passed down much more clumsily in practice. When Veronica's daughter breaks the sewing machine that Veronica inherited from her mother, she is briefly filled with rage – but is interrupted by the abrupt memory of breaking several rose-coloured teacups from her mother's youth and 'her own mother's voice in the 1950s, unrestrained, wailing, interminable, how *could* you, how *could* you.' The sentimental imperfection of this now-incomplete set of teacups becomes a touching symbol of the mother-daughter bond; the brash disregard of daughters towards the past and the earnest desire of mothers to pass down artefacts of their youth. While the story opens with the Veronica's daydreams of a rose-coloured tea party, the material reality is both more prosaic and more poignant.

Byatt (1936–2023) was one of the most celebrated British writers of her generation. Among her awards are the Booker Prize for *Possession* (1990) and the James Tait Black Memorial Prize for *The Children's Book* (2009), while she was made a Dame for services to literature in 1999.

Perhaps the most striking opening line in this collection is found in 'Love is Not a Pie' (1993) by Amy Bloom (b. 1953), an American writer and psychotherapist who has published four novels and five short-story collections:

※ ※ ※

In the middle of the eulogy at my mother's boring and heartbreaking funeral, I began to think about calling off the wedding.

The story then transports us back to a family holiday during which the daughter, Ellen, has a half-formed realisation about her mother. She and her sister Lizzie are 'always trying to figure her out', but there are years between revelation and a deeper understanding of her mother's life and unorthodox relationship. It represents another facet of many children's relationship with their parents: the discovery of their personhood beyond parenthood, and the time it takes to assimilate that.

The gradual understanding of a mother is more devastating in 'The Battle-Field' (1934) by Phyllis Bottome. Madeline is in her mid-thirties and considers herself to have a 'perfect maternal relationship' with her mother, who has nursed her through years of an unspecified lung disease. Eventually, Madeline takes up residence in a sanatorium. When the two women are separated for the first time, a knot of lies begins to unravel.

Arguably the darkest story in the collection, Bottome explores an instance where the closeness of the mother-daughter relationship becomes insular and co-dependent; sweetness becomes bitter; care becomes cloying. Phyllis Bottome (1884–1963) wrote many short stories and novels, including the spy thriller *The Lifeline* (1946) which, it has been suggested, directly influenced Ian Fleming in his creation of James Bond.

By contrast to Madeline's suffocatingly devoted mother, the mother in Tillie Olsen's 'I Stand Here Ironing' (1961) is sacrificial but – needing to work to provide as a single mother – unable to be a constant in the life of her daughter, Emily.

> She was a miracle to me, but when she was eight months old I had to leave her daytimes with the woman downstairs to whom she was no miracle at all.

Throughout the story, Olsen's mother chronicles a difficult childhood – beginning during the Great Depression and continuing into the Second World War – in which maternal love and sacrifice battle with material poverty. In the end, there is a quiet desperation from both mother and daughter, but they are determined to make the best of it.

Tillie Olsen (1912–2007) was an American writer who was part of the mid-century feminist movement, often highlighting the needs of working-class women. She only published three books during her lifetime: the Canadian writer Margaret Atwood has attributed this to the 'gruelling obstacle course' faced by many women writers of the demands of being a wife and mother.

Motherhood takes many forms, of course, and 'The Stepmother' (1928) highlights one variation. Esther King did not expect to marry but finds herself not only with a rather older husband, but also a stepdaughter, Ella. She believes her experience as a schoolteacher, indulging the infatuations of her pupils, will prepare her for such a relationship, but motherhood proves a completely different role. If the 'wicked stepmother' is the trope of fairy-tales, Esther experiences the prosaic friction of this adoptive role – and the return of a schoolgirl from her past doesn't make matters easier.

'The Stepmother' was published under the name 'Mary Arden', the pseudonym for Violet Murry, born Violet Le Maistre (1901–1931). She was the second wife of John Middleton Murry, married the year after his first wife, Katherine Mansfield, the renowned New Zealand short-story writer, died. Violet Murry was commonly considered to resemble Katherine Mansfield and, sadly, also died young of tuberculosis.

The final story in this collection takes place in a seemingly fantastical world of natural growth and creation. 'My Mother' (1983) by Jamaica Kincaid (b. 1949) follows a series of surreal vignettes, where female bodies and natural phenomena blur together as the connection between mother and daughter evolves.

It is a fitting story to end on because Kincaid includes so many facets of the connection between mother and daughter – from dependence to resentment, community to rejection, caution to intimacy. Yet, in Kincaid's telling, the whole world seems shaped from this evolving relationship, mythologising and abstracting the personal until the mother becomes something as fearsome and divine as mother nature herself.

Jamaica Kincaid is an Antiguan-American writer whose novels and stories often explore colonialism, race, gender and sexuality. She is also an avid gardener and has written extensively on the topic.

Every relationship between mother and daughter is unique, like any relationship between any parent and child, but the women writers in this volume have all captured something touching, profound, or amusing in that relationship that can speak to readers decades later.

Molly Thatcher, Editor
Simon Thomas, Consultant Editor

Publisher's Note

These stories, like the original novels reprinted in the British Library Women Writers series, were written and published, for the most part, from the 1910s to the 1950s. There are many elements of these stories which continue to entertain modern readers, however, in some cases there are also uses of language, instances of stereotyping and some attitudes expressed by narrators or characters which may not be endorsed by the publishing standards of today, and we acknowledge may continue to make uncomfortable reading for some of our audience. With this series, British Library Publishing aims to offer a new readership a chance to read some of the rare books of the British Library's collections in an affordable paperback format, to enjoy their merits and to look back into the world of the twentieth century as portrayed by their writers. It is not possible to separate these stories from the history of their writing and as such the stories are presented as originally published with minor edits made for consistency of style and sense. We welcome feedback from our readers, which can be sent to the following address: British Library Publishing, The British Library, 96 Euston Road, London, NW1 2DB.

Week-End

Richmal Crompton

Four o'clock. They'd be here any minute now. She went out into the little garden and stood there, motionless, hardly breathing, drawing the peace and quiet of it into her very soul. She felt guilty, as though she were taking a farewell of her lover till it would be safe for him to come to her again. It wasn't, of course, that she didn't adore them, that she didn't look forward to their coming all the week. Only—when she knew that they'd be here any minute, she always felt like this, always seemed to see the beloved brooding peace of the little place gather itself together, as it were, into a dim glamourous shape, take a quick leave of her, then turn to flee at the sound of their voices on the hill.

She heard the sound of their voices on the hill now, and went through the hall where the sunlight lay in splashes on the dark polished floor, and out into the front garden. She was always standing at the little green gate waiting for them when they came up the hill from the station. They expected it, and would have been vaguely distressed not to have found her there. They were very conventional, despite their ostentatious modernity. Bruce had been like that, too. ...

She heard them—eager, noisy, all talking together, before they came round the bend in the road that showed them to her. She could see them now—four light, athletic, girlish figures swinging up the hill, carrying suitcases. The tall one on the right must be the girl who worked in Celia's office. They'd said that they were going to bring her over the next time they came. Her name was Nancy Tibblits, and they called her Nibbles. They generally brought a friend home with them for the week-end, because the cottage could just be made to hold five with a little managing. If they'd lived in a house that would hold ten guests, they'd have brought eleven guests home with them for the week-end regularly, as a matter of course. Bruce had been like that, too... .

The three of them flung themselves upon her. They were still all talking together, and she couldn't hear what any of them said, but she caught the word Nibbles, and turned to the fourth girl with a welcoming smile.

"I'm so glad that you could come, dear," she said.

Nibbles laughed and said:

"Oh, I've been simply longing to come, looking forward to it all week."

She had the curious impression that Nibbles was welcoming her, trying to put her at her ease. She always felt like that with the girls' friends.

They were all over the house and garden now, shouting to each other from room to room, from the upstairs windows to the garden. It was lovely to have them all back with her again, to see with her own eyes that they were well and happy, and yet she felt breathless and bewildered. There seemed to be so many of them, and they all talked so loudly and at once. They worked in offices in London. Celia and Doreen shared a flat together, and Gwynneth shared one with a girl they called Cucumber, who generally went to her own home for the week-end.

They were ostensibly helping her to get the tea now, but of course it took twice as long as if she'd been left to get it alone. They were "ragging" each other, screaming with laughter, making exciting little discoveries in all the cupboards they opened.

"What's in this jar? Oh, candied peel. Have some candied peel, Nibbles. Don't you adore candied peel?"

"Oh, do look! Here's my old china mug. Yours is here, too, Celia. 'A present for a Good Girl.' Do you remember them. Let's get them out. Move that pile of plates and we can get to them."

"I'm going to bag this honey jar. It's just what we want for the flat."

Tea was ready at last, and they sat round the little gate-legged table in the dining-room, with the scent of the garden creeping in at the open window.

They were still all talking together, exchanging news about their work and their flats, discussing future plans and common acquaintances. She often wondered how they managed to hear each other.

As she sat there, smiling, silent, in the midst of the babel, it was as if one part of her yearned over them in motherly love while the other shrank from them almost in panic. It had been like that with Bruce, her husband, even before they were born....

Bruce, too, had been noisy and high-spirited, never quite happy without a crowd of noisy, high-spirited people around him. She had adored Bruce, but she had always felt like this with him. ... She glanced round at the table again. They were just like Bruce ... handsome, good-tempered, restless. She remembered how desperately she had longed that one of them might share her love of peace and solitude and books and quiet ways.... But they had all turned out like Bruce.... And she loved them, loved them fiercely, proudly, and was ashamed of the part of her that shrank from them. For they were good girls—kind, tender-hearted, honest ... like Bruce.

They came into the kitchen to help her wash up, but forgot

what they'd come for, and drifted out again to put records on the gramophone. They were in the drawing-room when she went back to them. They had moved the furniture against the walls. Celia was putting on records, Doreen and Nibbles were dancing, and Gwynneth had piled all the cushions on to the floor and was lying on them.

Gwynneth leapt to her feet, and seized her by the waist as she entered.

"Come on, Mums!" she said, and whirled her round the room.

She laughed and protested.

"Oh, darling, don't ... don't!"

Gwynneth released her after a few rounds, threw her into a chair and herself at her feet.

"Isn't she a pet?" she said to Nibbles, "and she's such an angel about having to live in the country like this. It is a shame. We all come down every week-end, of course, to stop her getting mopy. When we're millionaires we're going to get her a flat somewhere very posh—Sloane Street or Knightsbridge or somewhere like that."

"Darling, I *like* living in the country ..."

But it wasn't any use. She might tell them a dozen times a day that she liked living in the country, and it wouldn't make any impression on them. They were so kind and so good, and yet they simply couldn't see any other point of view than their own. Bruce had been like that. ... The divergence of his taste and hers had never troubled him because he had never realised it. The expression of any opinion of hers, different from his, would amuse him, make him find her "quaint," a "funny little thing," but he never took it seriously. And the girls were the same. They found her "quaint," too, and "a funny little thing," and they judged her, as they judged everyone, by their own standards, never modifying their ideas of her by anything that she said. It was rotten having to live buried in the country, and she was an angel about it. She knew that they came down to her here partly as a duty, to "cheer her up." If ever one of them came down alone, and found her leading the life she loved, sitting in her garden, reading, sewing, doing nothing in particular, filled with that serenity of happiness that quiet and silence always brought to her, she would report to the others that "Mother was getting mopy," and they would all come down in a body the next week-end to "cheer her up."

They had stopped the gramophone now, and were having a cushion fight. The house was full of screams and laughter. Celia and Gwynneth won, beating the other two gradually back into the little hall.

"What shall we do now?" said Celia, laughing and triumphant, tossing back her short hair.

Celia was more like Bruce than any of them. She seemed to see and hear Bruce in that laughing—"What shall we do now?" Bruce had always wanted to be "doing" something.

"Let's go for a walk before supper. Come along, Mums."

"I won't come, dear. I'll be getting the supper ready."

"Oh, you must come, darling. It'll do you good. We'll all help with the supper when we come in."

When they came in, they all ran round "helping." Celia and Doreen practised carrying plates all up their arms like waiters and broke two. Nibbles and Gwynneth held races on the carpet with the table-mats, seeing who could roll hers the farthest.

She got ready the supper as best she could, still trying to fight down that strange shrinking that their noisiness had always brought to her. ...

After supper it was quieter, but it was a quietness of whispered plots, of barely held-in-check excitement, a quietness broken by little screams of anticipatory delight. ... Creeping up and down stairs ... keeping "*caves*." They loved to play tricks upon each other. ...

She went to bed early, and Celia, who was sleeping in her room, said, "I'll be up soon, dearest. Don't stay awake for me."

She lay awake in the darkness listening to it all. Nibbles's scream when she opened her bedroom door and the wet sponge dropped on to her ... her shrieking pursuit of Gwynneth up and down the stairs. ... Doreen's delighted yells when she found the hairbrush in her bed. ... Occasionally one of them said "Hush! We mustn't disturb Mother." Finally they gathered in the room where Gwynneth and Doreen were sleeping, and talked there till half-past one. The sound of their voices and the smell of their cigarettes floated in to her as she lay in bed. Then Nibbles went to the little cupboard of a room where her bed was (it was about all that it would hold) and Celia came to hers.

"Hush!" she heard Celia say as she opened the door. "I don't want to wake Mother."

Celia undressed quickly, whistling under her breath, got into bed, and fell asleep at once.

She lay awake till sunrise. It seemed to her that the house and garden were frightened, and she had to stay awake to comfort them.

They began to get up at nine the next morning, but wandered about the house till eleven with practically nothing on. Nibbles, smoking a cigarette, dressed in tight navy blue woollen gym knickers, kept sliding down the balusters, her arms held wide apart. Celia and Doreen turned cartwheels in the hall, and tried to walk upstairs on their hands, collapsing on to every step with screams of laughter. Gwynneth, still in her pyjamas, put jazz band records on to the gramophone in the drawing-room, and stood in the doorway, shouting encouragement to the others.

At last they sat down to breakfast. Nibbles wore a sweater, but hadn't put a skirt over her gym knickers. Celia had a kimono over her pyjamas. Doreen and Gwynneth were more or less dressed.

In the middle of breakfast the church bells began to ring, and they saw people passing the gate on their way to church. Celia jumped up and said, "Come on, Nibbles ... let's shock them," and they stood in the front porch smoking cigarettes, Nibbles in her knickers and Celia in her kimono over her pyjamas. Only a few people saw them, and they looked merely amused, so at last they came in, disappointed, to finish their breakfast.

On the rare Sundays on which they didn't come down, she always went to the village church. The girls never went to church. They said that they disapproved of institutional religion and were quite unaware that they conscientiously governed their lives by rules taught them by institutional religion in their childhood. She knew it, and it amused her.

After breakfast Nibbles and Gwynneth had a race, each climbing one of the pine trees at the bottom of the garden, while the others cheered them from below. Then the rain drove them indoors, and they tobogganed downstairs on kitchen trays.

Once she heard Celia say to Doreen, "You can come down next week-end, can't you, Do?"

And then to Nibbles, "We always try to come down every week-end to cheer Mother up."

It was nearly three by the time they had finished lunch. Then, when she'd washed up, they all "helping," it was time to get the tea, and then quite suddenly they found that they must simply fly if they were to catch their train. They never thought of beginning to do anything till it was doubtful if they'd be able to do it in time. Bruce had been like that. ... She loved order and method and punctuality, and she had tried hard to make them love it, too, but it hadn't been any use.... Like Bruce, they hated to begin to do anything till it was almost too late. They loved to hurl themselves into trains just as they were starting off. It added a zest to life and kept them in that state of excitement that they loved. She had schooled herself not to "fuss," but she couldn't resist saying, "Children, if you're going by the usual train, hadn't you better—"

They greeted it with screams of delighted laughter.

"Isn't she sweet!"

"Darling, there's nearly half an hour."

"Nibbles, she always catches the train *before* the one she means to catch!"

"You *adore* stations, don't you, beloved?"

Smiling her faint, gentle smile, she managed to contain herself after that, though part of her was breathlessly packing for them and hurrying them down the hill to catch their train. And now she would always begin subconsciously to key herself up for the crescendo of the week-end. It was like an express train going through a station … louder … louder … louder … so that you'd think it couldn't possibly be any louder, and then—a thundering, deafening, incredible roar before it began to die away. … As a child that had been one of her worst nightmares, and the last few minutes of their visit always reminded her of it. For suddenly they were tearing up and down the stairs, flinging things into suitcases, shouting to each other frantically all over the house.

"I say, where are my pyjamas?"

"We'll *never* catch it."

"*Do* hurry, Do."

"This isn't my hairbrush. …"

"I saw it in the drawing-room."

"Where's that honey jar I bagged?"

"*Where* are my shoes?"

"Nibbles, here's your toothbrush."

"I say, we'll *never* do it!"

And then a sudden raid upon the garden. She tended her flowers and loved them dearly, and it always hurt her to see them hacked down anyhow with knives or fingers. They didn't really care for flowers, but it was the "thing" to take back a bunch of flowers from the country, and so they had to do it.

Then they besieged the store-cupboard, shouting to her all at the same time.

"Darling, we're taking some jam."

"May I have this tin of sardines, Mummie? It'll just go into my suitcase."

"Have you any lemon cheese, darling? Cucumbers does adore it so. Oh, yes! Here's some! Good!"

"I say, I've knocked over a tin of something. ... I haven't time to pick it up."

"I say, we'll *never* do it, you know. *Do* come on."

"Wait a *minute*. I must have two teaspoons. Mummie, where are the teaspoons? You don't mind, do you?"

"Currants! I *must* take some currants. ..."

They were still tearing up and down the stairs, forgetting things and dashing back for them, shouting to each other to hurry, saying that they'd simply never do it.

They were all down in the hall now, where the four parcels she had made up for them—each containing apples and a cake—stood upon the chest.

They snatched them up and hugged her,

"We've had a *perfect* time, precious. We'll be back next week-end. Don't let yourself get mopy. ..."

They were running headlong down the road towards the station, laden with parcels. Gwynneth was carrying her pyjama trousers in her hand because she'd lost them till the last minute, and hadn't had time to pack them. They all turned at the bend in the road to wave to her. Gwynneth waved her pyjama trousers. They screamed affectionate farewells as they disappeared.

The sound of their voices died away in the distance. She still stood at the gate waiting. ... Faintly in the distance came the sound of the train. ... They must have caught it, just caught it, as usual. ... She turned and walked slowly back to the little house. She stood in the hall for a minute, listening to the silence of it. Then, a tremulous smile upon her lips, she went to the garden, on which lay the still hush of twilight. She stood, eyes closed, lips still faintly smiling. At her heart was a radiant ecstasy, and beneath it a faint, half-unconscious sense of guilt.

They had gone, and her lover had come back to her. ...

Maternal Devotion

Sylvia Townsend Warner

"I was taught how to make tea by Professor Abernethy in Dresden. He always used an egg cup. Not that his name was Abernethy, or anything like it," Mrs Finch said to the young man who had come to call on her daughter. "It was more like Euston or Thompson."

As kittens bring in the mice that are too much for them to be finished off by the cat, Cordelia Finch had a habit of depositing any inconvenient suitors with her mother and leaving the rest to nature. When the Finches moved from London to Kent and their new neighbours hastened to call on them, the number of deposited suitors rose sharply. This one was a Mr Weatherby, who was locally expected to become a Member of Parliament when he had matured. Mrs Finch had told him that Cordelia was not at home, adding, with equal mendacity, that she hoped he would stay and have tea.

"I can't think why I should so persistently call him Abernethy," she continued. "He wasn't in the least like a biscuit."

"Some association of ideas, perhaps," Mr Weatherby suggested.

"I don't see how it can be, for I detest Abernethy biscuits, and he was such a kind old man. He used to be followed about by a cab."

After a slight pause, Mr Weatherby said, "Really?"

"His wife had an idea that his legs might give way suddenly," Mrs

Finch said. "He was well over ninety. Do you come of a long-lived family, Mr Weatherby?"

Mr Weatherby said guardedly that he had had an aunt.

"Do tell me about her," said Mrs Finch warmly.

"There isn't much to tell, really. She lived to be eighty and died of a stroke."

"What would you like to die of?" Mrs Finch asked. "I think, myself, there's a great deal to be said for a general atrophy, for if one has to be a nuisance, it's better not to be an active nuisance. Or would you prefer a sudden death? You might fall off a horse and be carried home dead on a five-barred gate. Do have some more cake."

"Thank you," said Mr Weatherby. "Why a five-barred gate?"

"It's usually the gate that's nearest, I believe. 'Do the thing that's nearest, Though 'tis dull at whiles,' you know. 'Helping when you meet them—'* That always seems to me such an extravagant piece of advice. Why should one help mad dogs over stiles? Why shouldn't they be able to run through underneath, as dogs in their senses do? I don't believe that even a mad dog would lose touch with reality to that extent. Or do you suppose that it really applies to idiot dogs who have lost the use of their legs, unlike Professor Abernethy? Scansion makes poets very servile. Though with a little ingenuity, and if you don't scorn classical diction, why not 'Helping when you meet them Idiot dogs o'er stiles'?"

"I should think it would be rather a waste of time. Besides"—Mr Weatherby's eye gleamed with the acumen of debate—"how could one help dogs if one didn't meet them?"

"Exactly! Or if there wasn't a stile? Must you drag the poor

---

* This passage uses a comedic misquotation of the poem 'The Invitation: To Tom Hughes' by Charles Kingsley (1856). The correct lines run: 'Do the work that's nearest, / Though it's dull at whiles, / Helping, when we meet them, / Lame dogs over stiles.'

creature along till you find one? I'm so glad you agree with me about poetry not interfering with one's behaviour. Poets should never give good advice unless it's of the most placid description, like not turning aside to view the braes of Yarrow, or '*Prends l'éloquence et tords-lui le cou.*' I suppose chairmen at political meetings never read Verlaine."

Mr Weatherby looked up as one who sees a momentary lighthouse through the storm. Mrs Finch smiled at him and swept on. "If I were a poet, I would keep myself entirely to sonnets and advise no-one. There are still a great many subjects without sonnets. Have you ever considered writing a sonnet sequence on the non-conforming churches? 'Stern Muggleton,' one of them might begin. And then you could have 'Equestrian Wesley' and 'Leave thou the babe unsprinkled till the work of grace has something-or-othered.'"

"Well, to tell you the worst, you know," Mr Weatherby said, "I don't read much poetry. I don't seem to be that sort of man."

"I expect you are influenced by it, all the same," Mrs Finch said. "Everyone is. Do you know that during Wordsworth's lifetime the population of England more than trebled itself?"

Mr Weatherby said that he supposed Wordsworth lived a long time.

"He died," said Mrs Finch, "at exactly the same age as your aunt."

There was a pause. Mrs Finch broke it. "In Russia, when there is one of these awkward silences, people account for it by saying that a fool has been born."

There was another pause. Mr Weatherby broke it. "Will your daughter hunt?" (Mr Weatherby, who had recently put on weight, had a horse to dispose of.)

"I assure you, Mr Weatherby, any hunting in this family will be done by me. I spend my life hunting. At this moment, I am hunting for—" Mrs Finch broke off and rummaged among the sofa cushions. "I had the list but I seem to have mislaid it," she said. "But I remember it began with a black bishop—do you play chess?—and

Mr Harley's hat. Do you know Mr Harley? He tunes pianos. Such a nice, sombre man. If you met him in a pink dressing gown, you wouldn't know him from an El Greco, and it was so unfortunate that he lost his hat somewhere about the place. And then there was my husband's briefcase. It had a corkscrew in it and some other things. And the last thing on the list was the fire extinguisher. It's one of those clever chemical ones—you give them a smart blow and they burst into spray. Are you afraid of fire? Fire breaking out in a lunatic asylum is one of my terrors. I wonder if you are sitting on it. No, no, please don't trouble. It will be none the worse, and anyhow by the time I find it, it will be out of date. Do you think this tea was made with boiling water? I don't."

Looking wistfully towards the window, Mr Weatherby said, "I suppose you garden quite a lot."

"I've got a little watering pot. But whenever I find time to use it, it's always raining. Are you good at gardening?"

"Well, no," Mr Weatherby said. "I spud up daisies sometimes. But my mother's frightfully keen on gardening. So was my old aunt. She gardened right up to the end."

Mrs Finch nodded sympathetically. "I'm always alarmed when I see people plunge into gardening. Still, if your mother enjoys it … Besides, there is the Fifth Commandment. I read right through the Ten Commandments the other day, and I was surprised to find how many of them I agreed with. But it would have saved a lot of talk, as well as being much lighter to carry, if Moses had just boiled them down to one compact little commandment—'Thou shalt not interfere.' I knew a Mrs Prothero who was perfectly devoted to gardening, and one day when she was being shown around a friend's garden she saw a weed and tried to pull it up. It happened to be a tight-rooted wolfsbane, and while she was tussling with it, something snapped and she went blind in one eye. Could you have a plainer warning against meddling?"

While Mrs Finch was relating this story, noises, strongly suggestive of the dangers of meddling, had broken out in the front hall—a crash, an urgent sizzling, angry words, and hurried footsteps. These were now followed by a steady swishing sound, apparently proceeding from the neighbourhood of the doorstep.

"I say—" said Mr Weatherby. Mrs Finch looked at him devoutly, as though the lightest word from him meant more to her than any of the noises, indoors and out.

"I say!" he repeated. From where he sat, Mr Weatherby could see a jet of high-pressured spray sweeping across the lawn.

The noises died away. A strong chemical smell remained, and grew stronger.

"I always feel so sorry for Angelo Domodossola," Mrs Finch said. She had given up waiting for Mr Weatherby's communication. "He, of course, was born blind, so he got about quite easily. One day, he went to see a friend. He walked right in and called, and as there was no answer, he sat down to wait. It was midwinter, and that bitter Neapolitan cold—you know how it gets into one's bones. At last, he decided to wait no longer. He put down his hand to grope for his hat and gloves and felt some-thing clammy. It was a pool of blood. The friend had been there all the time. He had cut his throat half an hour or so before. I've never felt easy going to call on anyone since, for it is absurd to say that these coincidences never happen twice, and though I am not blind, I am very inattentive. I am sure I could sit in a room with a corpse for hours before I noticed anything was wrong."

Mr Weatherby saw that where the spray had fallen, the grass was turning yellow.

"I suppose if one were really observant," Mrs Finch said, "one would constantly notice that something or other was a little wrong."

"'Where ignorance'—" Mr Weatherby began.

The door opened and a voice said, "Of all the damned, confounded places to put the damned thing in! Elinor!" Mr Weatherby rose to his feet as Mr Finch burst into the room.

"Sit down, sit down, Mr Weatherby," Mrs Finch commanded. "An old man's curse will do you no harm. Henry, this is Mr Weatherby."

"How do you do?" said Mr Finch. "Excuse me for being in this filthy state. I had to put out a fire extinguisher."

"Oh, have you actually found it?" Mrs Finch said. "Where was it, Henry? I hope the poor thing's all right."

"I should say it was in the pink of condition, my dear," Mr Finch replied. "Some obliging house mover had put it in my briefcase. The briefcase was on the top shelf of the hall closet. I began to pull it down, and as it wasn't properly closed, a great many things began to drop out. The extinguisher just missed my head but fell on its own, and came promptly into action. I think I have killed some of the roses—I had to aim the beastly stuff somewhere but your extinguisher is none the worse, I believe. I must go and wash. Do sit down, Mr Weatherby. It's all over now."

"Henry!" Mrs Finch called after him as he left the room. "Was the corkscrew—Oh, well, he will tell me later. Now, if I could find my list, I could scratch off the extinguisher and the briefcase in one blow. It's a comfort to find that extinguishers work so efficiently, isn't it? Though for the moment I suppose this one has nothing left to work with. Do you often move from one house to another, Mr Weatherby? It's a very strange experience, but I think if I fell into the way of it, I should enjoy it. It is so enlarging to the mind."

Having got to his feet, Mr Weatherby had remained there, and now said he really must be going. Mrs Finch, preceding him into the hall, uttered a glad cry. "Can that be Mr Harley's hat? And look at this! Isn't this odd?" She pointed to a framed and illuminated text, propped against the legs of a chair. The words of the text were "It is good for me that I have been in trouble."

"Unless Henry had it in college—he had some very queer things then, but of course he has changed a great deal since—I can't account for it," Mrs Finch said. "Perhaps it was in the house when we came, like the two rag dolls we found in the wine cellar, looking exactly like Sin and Death in *Paradise Unbound*. Is it *your* hat, Mr Weatherby? I do hope it's none the worse for being extinguished. Goodbye. I am so sorry Cordelia was out. You must come again."

At a safe interval after the door had closed, Cordelia Finch appeared carrying a teapot. "I thought I'd make some fresh tea," she said to her mother, "and I've got some more sandwiches. I thought you might need reviving. My gratitude no words can express, but perhaps a few deeds—What *has* Father been doing?"

The new tea was just being poured out when Mr Finch came in, smelling of soap, and asked, "Is that freshly made tea or that fellow's leavings?" Cordelia explained that the tea was freshly made. "Thank God!" Mr Finch said, and then, turning to his wife, he said, "Well, Elinor, what have you been doing all the afternoon?"

"First, I rearranged the poetry shelves," Mrs Finch said, "and then I had Cordelia's Mr Weatherby. Cordelia, darling, when you met him, could he talk of anything but his aunt?"

"I don't think he mentioned his aunt."

"Oh, well, no doubt she's died since. That would account for his depression," Mrs Finch said. "She must have meant a great deal to him. It was impossible to get him to talk about anything else."

THE VALUE OF BEING SEEN

INEZ HOLDEN

The mornings in Charles Street were like the last stages in producing a play before the opening night.

Mrs. Ascot had taken the house for the winter; there were frequent troubles with new servants and with tradesmen, who had no knowledge of Mrs. Ascot and naturally had doubts about her.

The telephone was going all the time, and though Mrs. Ascot had seen to it that three different newspapers were to make public the fact that she and her daughter Miss Daphne Ascot had taken this house for the winter, quite half the time it was friends of the family who had been living there before. Was it possible, Mrs. Ascot said to herself, that there were still such numbers in existence who did not see the newspapers? Daphne's schooling in England was at an end; she had been 'polished' in Paris, and her mother had come to the decision that it was time for her to give up being a schoolgirl and take her place in London society.

"My dear," she said, "it is quite time you came out."

Daphne had nothing to say about this because she did not ever have anything to say about anything; she would be no trouble; she would go quietly from dance to dance, in the same way as at school she had gone from room to room, and in Paris from the Louvre to Notre Dame and back.

Mrs. Ascot was of the opinion that it was only necessary to give her daughter the general idea, the keynote, of being a débutante.

"The important thing is to be seen," she said. "Keep in mind, Daphne, that débuts are not made in one night; whatever others may say, it takes weeks of hammering away."

Mrs. Ascot herself had undertaken all the work of organization, getting on the lists, getting into the society news, getting together the right young men, and keeping the wrong ones away. She would take care of the selection of Daphne's dresses, she would keep an eye on her talk and her friends, and she would give the papers a 'story' of Daphne.

It was hard to make Daphne into a story; more than a good newspaper man was necessary for it. Only Mrs. Ascot herself would be able to make anything out of such poor material.

Daphne's face was regular but uninteresting; her hair light and at all times in order, she was not short or tall, and she was not good or bad looking.

The day came for Daphne to go to her first débutante dance. She did not have to get ready because she was 'got ready'; two servants and Mrs. Ascot herself seemed to get her worked into her clothing with their hands as if she was an iced sweet being got ready for Lucullus; and as if that was not enough, they had to have an argument over the ornaments—which jewels she was to put round her neck, and how a somewhat foolish little bit of hair was to be placed. They all seemed pleased with their part in the work, because they all had the feeling that they had made something where before there had been nothing. Something dressed up to seem like a person had become a living débutante, and had now to be sent out among men and women, well taken care of.

Daphne herself, seated in her mother's automobile, gave no thought to anything. This was because she was not used to thought; in place of it, she was half conscious of things. She had no fixed ideas, only a quiet, deep-down feeling like one of the lower animals. In addition to this, her mother had said to her: "All you have to do is to be seen, and that is simple enough for any girl. I will do the rest."

And then suddenly Daphne was in the middle of it. It gave her a shock, made her come out of her normal half-sleeping condition; it was as if she had been walking unconsciously by the side of a deep river and someone had come up at the back of her and given her a push. There was the same ice-cold feeling, the fighting for breath, before making the decision to go on swimming and not to give up. Being a débutante was no amusement.

She seemed to be seeing hundreds of eyes, which had no separate existence—simply a mass of eyes like caviare among noses; they did not seem to be anyone's specially, they were only a great number of eyes, liquid and dead. So this was her first dance. Her mother's words about the value of being seen came into her mind, but these eyes did not seem to be looking at her. They seemed to be looking, not at anyone or anything, but only looking.

Daphne did not get on very well. Persons did their best for her; they took young men up to her, white, thin, young men still learning the rules, who seemed only to have a desire for food and drink, and made no secret of the sad fact that but for this they would not have come there at all.

Daphne had a feeling as if she had been pushed into the middle of some competition, and no one had made the rules clear to her. There was a garden at the back of the house where men and women who had been dancing together were walking; they seemed to be talking to one another without any trouble, but Daphne took it as probable that their talk was quite as stiff and unnatural as hers.

She went into the garden by herself, and when she saw her mother she was ready to go straight back to Charles Street.

"Certainly not," said Mrs. Ascot. "What an idea at your first dance! Get a young man and have a *dance* with him."

There were Japanese lights hanging in the garden. In Mrs. Ascot's opinion it was all very beautiful.

"My daughter was fearing that I would not be interested," she made clear to another mother, "but it gives me great pleasure to see young persons having a good time."

While she was talking, Daphne, who had been unable to get a young man, was crying in the dressing-room.

After this, Daphne went to a great number of dances. There were dances all the time; sometimes her mother made her go to two or three in one night, but though she was a good number of hours in the dressing-room doing nothing, she gave no sign of being happy or unhappy; she did not even have much dancing, because it was hard to get men to have dances with.

Daphne's existence went on. There were more dances, tea meetings, Lord's, Goodwood, helping with plays for good causes; the unending putting on of dresses and having pictures taken; Daphne went about in a group of other débutantes all the time. They had nothing of any interest to say to one another—only cries of approval, foolish little laughs, and accounts of dances fixed for the future. There was not a quiet minute, and through it all no one seemed to see Daphne. She was unconscious of herself, and she went on being unseen.

Though there was no point in her débutante existence, it did not come to an end. It had become an uninteresting, automatic business without any purpose and which she was unable to put a stop to because she had no strong desire for anything. She had no memory of the past and she saw no future; there was nothing, only this automatic being a débutante.

Mrs. Ascot no longer went with her daughter to all the dances, because she said that there were times when mothers were not desired, so the old woman who had taken care of Daphne as a baby went with her in the automobile, waiting all night in the dressing-room ready to go back with her again.

"There will be no driving with young men for *my* daughter," Mrs. Ascot said; and it was no use for Daphne to say to her mother that in her mind there had been no question of driving anywhere with any young man.

Sometimes when Daphne got back late, she was questioned by Mrs. Ascot to see if she had had a good time, and she would give the same untrue answer, without any sign of interest, "Yes, mother; it was a beautiful dance." But the strange thing was that whenever Mrs. Ascot gave her daughter's opinion of any special dance, her friends said in surprise. "Oh, was your girl there? I did not see her." Mrs. Ascot was unhappy that Daphne had not been more of 'a noise,' but took comfort from the thought that while one person was getting some food another was dancing and it was simple enough to go through a night in this way without seeing quite everything.

But Daphne herself was unable to keep from noting the fact that her friends were getting more and more uncertain about her; no one ever seemed able to keep her name in mind; frequently she said something and got no answer, and when she said it over again they gave a little jump as if it had been a sudden voice coming out of the dark.

And then one night at a dance where Daphne was seated by herself at the table, with persons all round her who were not talking to her, she saw a very beautiful girl in the doorway looking for a place where she would be able to take a seat and get some food.

Beautiful girls were 'here to-day and gone to-morrow,' and Daphne did not give much attention to her. She went on quietly with her ice. And then she saw that the beautiful débutante was coming near her table. The others at the table gave a cry of, "Here you are, Gloria; here's a seat," pointing at Daphne's, and if she had not got quickly out of the way the girl would have taken a seat on top of her.

Then she was conscious what had taken place. It had been going on for some time. She was no longer able to be seen. She was nothing more now than the shade of a débutante.

After this, strange persons frequently gave her a sudden touch and seemed surprised, so that she got quite quick at getting out of the way.

Mrs. Ascot was quite unconscious of the sad change which had overtaken her daughter. She did not give much attention to Daphne, because she was certain in her mind that till her daughter got married she would be there. She only had a desire for others to see her.

"Don't get overlooked," she said. "It is the worst of all possible errors for a débutante to make."

"All right, mother," was Daphne's answer, in her uninteresting, feeble voice.

Daphne was conscious that she was still a little more than a shade. Sometimes two or three persons saw her in one day, and the change had been so slow that the servants were not conscious of it. All the house did its work on a dead, automatic system; the footman and driver were so used to taking the daughter of the house out on these journeys every night that it was all the same to them if she was there or not. When the automobile door was shut, they took it that she was inside, and when she said "Goodnight," it was clear to them that she had got out of the automobile.

The old woman's eyes were getting so feeble that the fact that she was unable to see and that Daphne was unable to be seen were the same thing to her, and she had no idea that anything strange had taken place.

One night the old woman got a bad cold and Daphne, seeing her chance, made her mother a request to let her have her meal in bed in place of going out to a dance, but Mrs. Ascot only gave her daughter a long look like a shocked bird and said:

"Your meal in bed! Well! When I was as old as you, I took the greatest pleasure in dances. Truly, it does put a mother off. Here am I working hard to get you all these dances, and the only reward one has is this foolish suggestion that you might have a meal in bed. Naturally you will have to go to the dance. If you don't, 'they' will have the idea you are no longer on the best lists. And no one ever sees Nanny, so you will have to say that she is sleeping in the dressing-room as she generally does."

"All right, mother," said Daphne's automatic voice, and she went off to the dance.

When she got there, she took her shade-like way up the steps into the dance-room, but she was surprised at the look of the room. It was not like a débutantes' dance; no one seemed to have much desire to be on the floor; they were all resting on long seats, drinking, smoking, and kissing, long and frequently, but all the time coldly. They were dressed in strange clothing, a number of them as sailors, and others had the look of having very quickly put on any clothing they were able to come across. Two or three persons were dancing by themselves, sometimes running into one another, but not troubling to come to a stop or say anything. And though she was conscious that no one was able to see her, she was happier because the room was so dark and so full of smoke that she was unable to see them very clearly.

At first it seemed to Daphne that it was like being dead, and then it seemed like walking through Selfridge's in the crush, with no idea what to get; and at last she was conscious that it was in every detail like, what it in fact was, a Bohemian night—the sort of thing the débutantes had a great desire to go to and which they were ordered by their mothers to keep away from, the sort of place where anyone might make love or get the worse for drink, or get into a fight.

Daphne took a seat to have a look round and made the discovery that she was on top of a fat woman dressed in colour-printed cotton pyjamas. She got up quickly, but the woman had gone to sleep and made no motion. Daphne had the feeling that these persons were like her in some ways, because they seemed as if they had been doing the same thing for nights and nights, and would probably keep it up till they went slipping away for ever. Some of them seemed so old that she had an idea they were not far from that happy ending.

Daphne saw a young man half out of the window making a great noise, and ready to take a jump into the street. No one gave any attention but Daphne herself, who had no idea that he did this every night. She put her head out of the window to say something to him and make him come back, but because she was unable to be seen he did not see her, and he was very conscious that voices which were not there frequently came to his ears in the same way as he saw rats in whose existence his friends had no belief. If the voice had an owner, then it was not important if he gave the person he saw in his mind a push.

"Go away," he said, and gave Daphne a blow, which sent her down into the street under the window.

It did not seem that death was coming to her. She had not ever taken a look forward, not ever seen herself dead in her mind. Her only idea was that because the old woman was ill, the complete automatic machine which was Charles Street in the winter had gone wrong. The footman had been given the wrong house and Daphne had got into a Bohemian dance, where, like most of the other persons, her company had not been requested. And because of this things were taking place, strange things. Nothing was working out as had been designed. She had doubts about how she was going to make it all clear to her mother, how it would be possible for her to say, "You see, mother, I am a shade—and have been for some time; and because he was unable to see me, this young man gave me a push and I had a fall into the street." No, it was not possible to say a thing like that to a woman like Mrs. Ascot. Daphne was conscious that it was impossible, and then a minute after, she was not conscious of anything. The street was no longer a street, the Bohemians were only a half-memory of a sleep experience; she had no memory of being a shade; she had no memory of anything at all.

The dance in the room at the top went on and on; a number of those present had nowhere to go, and others, not desiring to go back to a place where there was nothing going on, had by this time no idea where their houses were. There was nothing for them now but one long, unending night out.

Psalms

Jeanette Winterson

If you've ever tried to get a job as a tea-taster you will know as intimately as I do the nature of the preliminary questionnaire. It has all the usual things: height, weight, sex, hobbies new and old, curious personal defects, debilitating operations, over-long periods spent in the wrong countries. Fluency, currency, contacts, school tie. Fill them in, don't blob the ink and, if in doubt, be imaginative.

Then, on the last page, before you sign your name in a hand that is firm enough to show spirit, but not enough to show waywardness, there is a large empty space and a brief but meaningful demand.

You are to write about the experience you consider to have been the most significant in the formation of your character. (You may interpret 'character' as 'philosophy' if such is your inclination.) This is very shocking, because what we really want to talk about is that time we saw our older sister compromised behind the tool shed, or the time we very deliberately spat in the communion wine.

When I was small, I had a tortoise called Psalms. It was bought for me and named for me by my mother in an effort to remind me continually to praise the Lord. My mother had a horror of graven images, including crucifixes, but she felt there could be no harm in a tortoise. It moved slowly, so I could fully contemplate the wonders of creation in a way that would have been impossible with a ferret. It wasn't cuddly, so that I wouldn't be distracted as I might with a dog, and it had very little visible personality, so there was no possibility of us forming an intimate relationship as I might with a parrot. All in all, it seemed to her to be a satisfactory pet. I had been agitating for a pet for some time. In my head I had a white rabbit called Ezra that bit people who ignored me. Ezra's pelt was as white as the soul in heaven but his heart was black …

My mother drew me a picture of a tortoise so that I would not be too disappointed or too ecstatic. She hated emotion. I hoped that they came in different colours, which was not unreasonable since most animals do, and, when they were all clearly brown, I felt cheated.

"You can paint their shells," comforted the man in the shop. "Some people paint scenes on them. One chap I know has 26 and if you line 'em end to end in the right order you got the Flying Scotsman pulling into Edinburgh station."

I asked my mother if I could have another twelve so that I could do a tableau of the last supper, but she said it was too expensive and might be a sin against the Holy Ghost.

"Why?" I demanded as the man left us arguing in front of the gerbils. "God made the Holy Ghost, and he made these tortoises, they must know about each other."

"I don't want the Lord and his disciples running round the garden on the backs of your tortoises. It's not respectful."

"Yes, but when sinners come into the garden they'll be taken aback. They'll think it's the Lord sending them a vision." (I imagined the heathen being confronted by more and more tortoises; they weren't to know I had thirteen, they'd think it was a special God-sent tortoise that could multiply itself.)

"No," said my mother firmly. "It's Graven Images, that's what. If the Lord wanted to appear on the backs of tortoises he'd have done it already."

"Well can I just have two more then? I could do The Three Musketeers."

"Heathen child," my mother slapped me round the ears. "This pet is to help you think about our Saviour. How can you do that if you've got The Three Musketeers staring up at you?"

The man looked sympathetic, but he didn't want to get involved so we packed up the one tortoise in a box with holes and went to catch the bus home. I was excited. Adam had named the animals, now I could name mine. "How about The Man in the Iron Mask?" I suggested to my mother who was sitting in front of me reading her *Band of Hope Review*. She turned round sharply and gave a little screech.

"I've cricked my neck, what did you say?"

I said it again. "We could call it Mim for short, but it looks like it's a prisoner doesn't it?"

"You are not calling that animal The Man in the Iron Mask, or anything for short, you can call it Psalms."

"Why don't I call it Ebenezer?" (I was thinking that would match Ezra.)

"We're calling it Psalms because I want you to praise the Lord."

"I can praise the Lord if it's called Ebenezer."

"But you won't, will you? You'll say you forgot. What about the time I bought you that 3-D postcard of the garden of Gethsemane? You said that would help you think about the Lord and I caught you singing 'On Ilkley Moor Baht 'at'."

"Alright then," I sulked. "We'll call it Psalms."

So we did, and Psalms lived very quietly in a hutch at the bottom of the garden and every day I went and sat next to him and read him one of his namesakes out of the Bible. He was an attentive pet, never tried to run away or dig anything up, my mother spoke of his steadfastness with tears in her eyes. She felt convinced that Psalms was having a good effect on me. She enjoyed seeing us together. I never told her about Ezra the demon bunny, about his ears that filtered the sun on a warm day through a lattice of blood vessels reminiscent of orchids. Ezra the avenger didn't like Psalms and sometimes stole his lettuce.

When my mother decided it was time for us to go on holiday to Llandudno she was determined to take Psalms with us.

"I don't want you being distracted by Pleasure," she explained. "Not now that you're doing so well."

I was doing well; I knew huge chunks of the Bible by heart and won all the competitions in Sunday School. Most importantly, for an evangelical, I was singing more, which you do, inevitably, when you're learning Psalms. On the train my mother supplied me with pen and paper and told me to make as many separate words as I could out of Jerusalem. My father was dispatched for coffee and she read out loud interesting snippets from her new paperback, *Portents of the Second Coming*.

I wasn't listening; practice enabled me to pour out the variations on Jerusalem without even thinking. Words slot into each other easily enough once sense ceases to be primary. Words become patterns and shapes. Tennyson, drunk on filthy sherry one evening, said he knew the value of every word in the language, except possibly 'scissors'. By value he meant resonance and fluidity, not sense. So while my mother warned me of the forthcoming apocalypse I stared out of the window and imagined that I was old enough to buy my own Rail Rover ticket and go off round the world with only a knapsack and a penknife and a white rabbit. A white rabbit? I jumped a little at this intrusion into my daydream. Ezra's pink eyes were gleaming down at me from the frayed luggage rack. Ezra wasn't invited on this trip, I had been determined to control him and make him stay behind. In the box next to me I felt Psalms fidgeting. My mother was oblivious.

"Just think," she said enthusiastically. "When the Lord comes back the lion will lie down with the lamb."

But will the rabbit come to terms with the tortoise?

Like Psalms, I was feeling nervous, as one would when one's fantasy life gets out of control. Ezra's eyes bored into my soul and my own black heart. I felt transparent, the way I do now when I meet a radical feminist who can always tell that I shave my armpits and have a penchant for silk stockings.

"I'm trying to be good," I hissed. "Go away."

"Yes," continued my mother, all unknowing. "We'll live naturally when the Lord comes back, there'll be no chemicals or aerosol deodorants. No fornicating or electric guitars." She looked up sharply at my father. "Did you put saccharine in this coffee? You know I can't drink it without." My father smiled sheepishly and tried to placate her with a packet of Bourbons, which was a mistake because she hated anything that sounded foreign. I remembered how it had been when my auntie had come back from Italy and insisted on having us round for pasta. My mother was suspicious and kept turning it over with her fork and saying how much she liked hot pot and carrots. She didn't mind natives so much or people who lived in the jungle and other hot places because she felt they couldn't help it. Europe, though, was close enough to Britain to behave properly and, in not behaving properly, was clearly perverse and due to be rolled up when the Lord came back. (In the Eternal City there will be no pasta.)

I tried to distract myself from her gathering storm by concentrating on the notices in our carriage. I took in the exhortation to leave the train clean and tidy and felt suitably awed by the dire warnings against frivolously pulling the communication cord. Ezra began to chew it. Tired and emotional, though fondly imagining we shared a common ground other than the one we were standing on, we reached our boarding house at nightfall and spent the holiday in various ways. One morning my mother suggested we take Psalms with us to the beach.

"He'll enjoy a change of air."

I hadn't seen Ezra for a couple of days otherwise I might have been more alive to the possibilities of catastrophe. We set off, found a patch that wasn't too windy, said a prayer and my father fell asleep. Psalms seemed comforted by the sand beneath his feet and very slowly dug a very small hole.

"Why don't you take him to that rock in the breakers?" My mother pointed. "He won't have seen the sea before." I nodded, and picked him up pretending I was Long John Silver making off with booty. As we sat on the rock sunning ourselves a group of boys came splashing through the waves, one of them holding a bow and arrow. Before my eyes he strung the bow and fired at Psalms. It was a direct hit in the centre of the shell. This was of no matter in itself because the arrow was rubber-tipped and made no impression on the shell. It did make an impression on Psalms, though, who became hysterical and standing on his back legs toppled over into the sea. I lunged down to pick him out but I couldn't distinguish between tortoise and rocks. If only my mother had let me make him into one of The Three Musketeers I could have saved him from a watery grave. He was lost. Dead. Drowned. I thought of Shelley.

"Psalms has been killed," I told my mother flatly.

We spent all afternoon with a shrimping net trying to find his corpse, but we couldn't and at six o'clock my mother said she had to have some fish and chips. It was a gloomy funeral supper and all I could see was Ezra the demon bunny hopping up and down on the prom. If it had not been for my father's devotion and perseverance in whistling tunes from the war in a loud and lively manner we might never have recovered our spirits. As it was, my mother suddenly joined in with the words, patted me on the head and said it must have been the Lord's will. Psalms's time was up, which was surely a sign that I should move onto another book of the Bible.

"We could go straight onto Proverbs," she said. "What kind of pet would be proverbial?"

"What about a snake?"

"No," she refused, shaking her head. "Snakes are wily, not wise."

"What about an owl?"

"I don't want an owl in my room. Owls are very demanding and besides when your Uncle Bert parachuted into the canal by mistake, it was an owl I saw just before I got the telegram."

Death by water seemed to be a feature of our family, so why not have something that was perpetually drowned? "Let's get some fish, they're proverbial, and they'll be quiet like Psalms was, and they'll remind us of the Flood and our own mortality." My mother was very taken with this, especially since she had just eaten a fine piece of cod. She liked it when she could experience the Bible in different ways.

As for me, I was confronted with my own black heart. You can bury what you like but, if it's still alive when you bury it, don't look for a quiet life. Is this what the tea board wants to know about? Is it hoping to read of tortoises called Psalms?

I don't believe it. They must have an identikit picture of what constitutes a suitable forming experience, like playing quarterback in the school team and beating Wales, or saving a rare colony of worker bees from extinction.

My mother bought some brown ink in Llandudno and sketched Psalms on a few square inches of stiff card. She caught his expression very well, though I still feel the burden of being the only person who has ever seen what emotion a tortoise can express when about to drown. Such things are sobering and stretch down the years. I could have saved him, but I felt he limited my life. Sometimes I take out the sketch and stare at his mournful face. He was always mournful, though I think that was a characteristic of the breed because I have never met a jubilant tortoise. On the other hand, perhaps I never made him happy. Perhaps we were at emotional odds like Scarlett O'Hara and Rhett Butler. Perhaps a briny end was better than a gradual neglect. I ponder these things in my heart. My mother, always philosophical in her own way, enjoyed a steady stream of biblical pets: the Proverbial fish, Ecclesiast the hen who never laid an egg where we could find it, Solomon the Scotch terrier and, finally, Isaiah and Jeremiah, a pair of goats who lived to a great age and died peacefully in their pen.

"You can always depend on the prophets," declared my mother whenever anyone marvelled at the longevity of her goats. The world was a looking glass for the Lord—she saw him in everything. Though I do warn her, from time to time, never to judge a bunny by its pelt....

The End of the Fairy Tale

Maude Egerton King

She was entirely fashionable in everything save her motherhood, which still bore faint traces of its kinship with that of human mothers and the beasts of the field. For instance, although she generally forgot, she never regretted her only child's existence, and sometimes in rare lulls between her romps and frivolities she found the child as amusing a pastime as ping-pong on wet Sunday afternoons.

During that day on which the smart American widow was to dine her and a handful of congenials at the Savoy *en route* for the Empire, came a wire announcing the illness of her hostess. Then the big London house was moved at its two extremes, the kitchen depths sending up their grumble, that "she" was dining at home after all, to the nursery heights; with the result that the little Aurelia, reckless with sudden hope, eluded her nurse and the household law, hurried downstairs (right foot, right foot, right foot foremost all the way down, for the stairs were steep and her legs had only had five years to grow in) and entered the drawing-room in her nursery overall. There, to the childish eyes, the dearest and most beautiful lady in the world was sitting in a low chair near a tiny tea-table, and a long, straight man, who bore his eyeglass bravely like a pain, was filling up his glass from a siphon.

"Mother," said Aurelia, wondering if they heard her thumping heart, "you're not going out after all: so please be with me all this evening, and please put me to bed." And having come thus far in her unheard-of and desperate adventure, the mite could not be bribed away except with the given promise.

At half-past six the mother came upstairs; and now, as will often happen, a long neglect was followed by a sudden access of care.

"Are these the warmest night-socks the poor child has? And are those pyjamas thoroughly aired?" she inquired of the nurse.

For answer the woman swept the little silken garments off the fender rail and gave them her in contemptuous silence. She had, to the best of her personal and class ability, mothered the little girl for three years past. She had nursed her through croup and scarlet fever; she had made her clothes, adding the little unnecessary embroideries and fine tuckings that mean no less than love in the busy worker; she had as conscientiously frightened her with religion when naughty as she had dosed her with physic when ill; and in her own estimation there was very little that anyone could teach her about children, not even doctors, certainly not aunts, and least of all a lady who hardly ever saw her child save in her prettiest clothes and best behaviours.

"Does she still have such cold little feet?" said the mother, pulling off Aurelia's stockings.

"*I* have never known her have cold feet since *I* was here," replied the nurse.

"Well, she's certainly in better condition than she was when last I gave her a bath."

The nurse put up her eyebrows and went on tidying the room: what else than a bettering of condition was to be expected of a child in *her* charge?

"And how much bigger!" said the lady, still intent upon ingratiating herself with this important person.

"Yes, madam," said the nurse dryly, knowing herself far too valuable for dismissal. "You see she's had time to grow."

The mother made no further overtures, but devoted herself to the little girl; and nurse, whose contempt was mingled with jealousy, retired from the room, with the air of one who knows herself invaluable yet not valued, needed yet not desired, to sit nursing her feelings and darning little socks in her fireless bedroom rather than in the well-warmed linen-room next door.

Then began a great frolicking in the bath, which continued till the room was splashed from side to side.

"Oh, what will nursie say?" laughed the mother.

"I don't care!" sang out Aurelia, and wet as she was she plumped herself down on her mother's lap and hugged her.

"My gown!" cried the lady; but the mischief was done and one might as well enjoy the joke.

"I don't care for anything to-night," cried Aurelia. "Because I'm so dreffly happy. Oh, mother, can I sleep in your bed to-night?"

This was a rare pleasure, only granted to the little girl on birthdays and other such blue moons. And even pleasure is a poor name for the feeling that filled Amelia's heart when she entered the silken chamber and lay in the wonderful bed, where the little golden angels (for that was how Aurelia thought of the winged Loves) held up the gauzy curtains, and all the lights of the room seemed filtering through rose-leaves. A poor name, too, for her feeling when she woke in the night, and, remembering the company she was in, stretched out a little hand to make sure; or for the feeling which kept her—a fidgety, chattering creature from 6 a.m. onwards as a rule—lying quite still in the morning in that rose-and-fairy-land, as still as ever she sat in church and much, much happier, until such time as nurse came and fetched her away from her sleeping mother's side. And so, "Let me sleep in your bed to-night," said little Aurelia, coaxing all she knew.

"Well, just this one time you shall," said the mother, intent on fulfilling her duties to the uttermost since she was in the mood and they so pleasant. Aurelia whooped and danced about with almost as great a din as when she succeeded in dislodging the Boers (Ada, the sewing-maid) from their fortified kopje (the nursery sideboard); and then, quite out of breath, she tumbled into her mother's lap again.

The child's joy was so flattering and so refreshing that the mother found herself wondering why women were not better mothers than most of them were. This sort of thing was really great fun, and, unlike most fun, there wasn't any harm in it. She felt quite grateful to Mrs. Van Troden for going down with the influenza.

"And what's more," she went on, with further quickening of innocent desires and good resolutions, "what is more—but come, button up your dressing-gown and let's draw close to the fire!—what's more, you shall sleep there to-morrow night as well."

"Oh!" sighed Aurelia, and leaned against her mother. She could not shout or jump for joy any more; her happy heart was like an overladen honey-bee.

"And besides that, I've a wonderful plan in my head," continued her mother. The child sat up. "A plan for a lovely treat; indeed, I think I've got plans for a hundred treats," she said lavishly, smiling and looking deep into Aurelia's round eyes. It was worth being lavish to arouse such shining love and worship as there she saw; and, it is only fair to add that, as her promises slipped out, she believed in them as faithfully as the child. "What would you say if some day, when the spring comes, you and I, just you and I together, run right out into the country on the motor, and go into the woods and see primroses growing?—When I was a little girl like you, my home was set among woods, Aury.—And we'd just be gipsies together, you and I, and take our food with us, and sit on the ground and pick flowers, and go home quite late in the evening. Shall we, dear?"

"Let's! Let's! oh, let's!" cried Aurelia, emphasising with hugs. "And then? Then there's the *summer:* what shall we do when *that* comes? And then there's the *autumn;* and then there's next *winter.* Why, we shall have time for heaps and heaps of treats, shan't we?"

"But if I try to tell you all the treats I have in mind," said the mother, "we shall never get to bed!"

"*We* shall never get to bed?" exclaimed the child. "Will you come too, then, when I go? or will you come *quite* soon after? Do! do! then we can go to sleep together. I have never done this in all my life, in—all—my—life! Oh, do!"

Her mother had not intended this, but, filled with an unwonted sense of well-doing in this kingdom of love and innocency into which she had strayed, she willingly yielded yet further to the will of its queen.

"You funny little soul!" she said; "it isn't eight o'clock! Still, if you're so keen about it I'll come to bed ever so early—I won't even go down to dinner," she added, every moment driven to further extravagances by the long arrears of mothering in her heart. "I'll get Pinkney to bring me a cup of soup up here and then come straight to bed."

"Really and truly? Promise! Oh, you dearest!" During the hug that followed the mother found herself considering the best possible way of dropping Mrs. Van Troden, unless she would condescend to explain that *man* who was always there: but then there came to her mind an old proverb about the inadvisability of throwing stones for those who live in houses of glass, and she tried to dismiss the subject from her thought.

"I hope you always say your prayers, Aurelia," she said gravely, smoothing her hair.

"Yes, I do; I say them just after my night-socks, so that's now," said the child. Straightway she knelt down, asking God to bless her mother, and her daddy in South Africa, and bring him home safe, and to bless nursie, and to make herself a good girl. Amen. And then, standing up and putting her hands behind her, she carefully repeated a trite hymn all about lambs and little children and Jesus Christ, which somehow brought the tears to her mother's eyes.

"Little Aurelia," she said, drawing her cheek against her own, "why don't you sometimes say, 'God make daddy and mother good,' as well as 'make me a good girl,'—eh?"

"Because you're grown up!" was the prompt reply: nothing more, because it was such a well-known fact that it was only children who were naughty.

The mother found herself considering the possibility of moving out of her own particular glass house—nay, the desirability too.

Aurelia's cup of joy was not yet full, for a fairy-tale was promised, to be told before the nursery fire while the fire in the rosy room was burning up. It was long since the mother had told a fairy-tale, longer still since she had read one. In her desire to pay a long-owed debt of "good influence," she wove a very threadbare story round about a whole bundle of obvious and naked morals. It was a poor bit of art, but Aurelia listened greedily and loved it all, although therein were allegorised so many of her pitiful little sins and weaknesses. The *dramatis personæ* were a Princess, a Bad Fairy, and a Good Fairy. As the Bad Fairy arrived in time for the christening and the good one did not, the poor child was morally handicapped through early childhood, and the description of her unregenerate condition was full of home-thrusts and unmistakable meanings; but, with the gradual mastery of the Good Fairy, the Princess became a person of immaculate morals and behaviour, who never came downstairs without politely asking permission, and certainly never in a dirty frock; never was selfish, asking her mother to play with her when she was busy or had a headache; never was cheeky to her nurse, and would have died rather than slap a sewing-maid; never left her porridge, nor refused to eat crusts. ...

"But *I do* finish up my porridge now, and I *don't* leave my crusts," said the child in disappointed astonishment. "Don't you 'member, how I tried and tried, and then I didn't leave it any more, and so then you gave me Doll Dinah? Don't you *'member?*" It had been such an epoch in the little life.

"Now, how naughty of me to forget!' said her mother. "Of course you did." For a moment the idea of preaching to this generous, loving and innocent creature became an absurdity and indecency.

But, "Go on, please," coaxed Aurelia; and so the story went forward, relating how happy the Princess's mother became in seeing her little girl so good; until the listener again interrupted with, "I *will* try to be like the Princess. I *will* try to give my strawberries and cream to poor beggar children. I *will* try and not be selfish any more; and even if I have the loveliest doll in the world—like Doll Dinah even," she said, shutting her eyes tight and nodding her head in great jerks to emphasise her determination—"I *will* try to give it to somebody else, if you like. I believe I'm not going to do anything naughty or unkind any more all my life for ever and ever, and be just like you, mother dear!" She opened her eyes and drew breath. "Well, and what did the Bad Fairy be able to do?" she went on. "I don't think the Bad Fairy could do much, because the Good Fairy was so awfully strong, wasn't she, don't you believe?"

"Well, I'm just coming to that," said the mother. "The Bad Fairy—"

Someone knocked at the door, and a maid entered. "Major Morrison is here," she said.

"Major Morrison?" repeated the mother, with a sense of shock and disappointment.

Aurelia's hold became a clutch. "You won't go, will you?" she said, a little sternly. "You promised me."

"My dear heart, I didn't know when I promised that—"

The child flashed round on the maid with blazing cheeks. "Please tell Major Morrison to go away," she said imperiously.

"Hush, Aurelia! how dreadfully rudely you speak! I don't want to leave you, but I mustn't be rude or unkind just for your pleasure's sake, must I?"

"Why must you see him?" the child pleaded tremulously. "Why must you? Why?"

The superior maid waited in chill and immovable silence.

"I'll come," said the mother, flushing a little, and looking at her above the child's head.

The superior maid turned to go.

"Stop," said Aurelia, with heaving chest: "just ask Major Morrison to wait till we've finished the fairy-tale. And then after that," she continued imploringly, "how soon will you come upstairs to go to sleep with me?"

The maid closed the door.

"Now, my sweetheart," said the mother, "I want you to be the most sensible little Princess in the world. I can't finish the story now, and I can't come up as early as I had hoped to do; but very soon after you are asleep, I—"

Aurelia jumped off her lap. "That man is a big, cruel beast, and I hate him, I hate him, I hate him!" she cried, stamping her foot; then she burst into passionate sobbing.

Her criticism was juster than she knew, and, for that very reason, painful and unwelcome to her mother's ears.

"Hush, hush, Aury! If you loved me you would try to love my friends." She took her on her lap again and soothed her into some sort of resignation; then she suddenly laid her head on the little shoulder. "You make me very unhappy, Aury," she said; and it was perfectly true, but this was by reason of her own and not Aurelia's shortcomings. Why had this visit happened this peaceful, beautiful evening? It filled her with a sense of unseemly intrusion; it jarred and put her out of tune with itself and herself and her new-found peace as well. And yet, a very little later, after promising to come back and show herself before going down to the drawing-room, she left her child and went away to dress. A passionate woman who doubts her power of holding is the most enslaved creature on earth.

Something had certainly gone wrong with the world to-night. Aurelia was conscious of having misbehaved herself just when she meant to be, and thought herself, as good as any Princess! She sat alone by the nursery fire, wondering ruefully, and holding on to the one fragment left of her wrecked but glorious evening: her mother would come and show herself when dressed, and Aurelia loved to see how white she looked against the soft, black, misty stuff, with bright things glittering like frost in her dark hair. But apparently the mother forgot all about it, and went downstairs without coming near the nursery; and at nine o'clock nurse found the forsaken child still waiting.

"So that's the way she does it, does she?" sniffed the woman. But she wrapped her up warmly and carried her tenderly enough over to the far-off rose-coloured chamber.

"Do you mean my mother?" said Aurelia, with the threatening of tears. "Please don't say 'she': it's rude."

There was a soft rustling outside the door, and then Aurelia's mother came in, very pale, brilliant-eyed, and still wearing the dress which she had worn in the nursery.

Aurelia stared, and then, "Mother! mother!" she cried, quite suddenly wideawake, suddenly comforted, suddenly overjoyed; and she jumped up and down until the glass and silver knick-knacks jingled.

"That will do, nurse," said the lady, speaking a little breathlessly, as though she had sped up the stairs.

Patting the clinging child's head, she waited for the astonished woman's departure, which was as deliberate as curiosity and jealousy could make it. When the door at last closed upon her unwilling exit, the mother lifted the child into her lap.

"I was so dreadfully afraid you'd be asleep, Aury," she said, as if this had been a matter of life and death: "I want you—I want you—I want you!"

Hugged to her bosom as she was, the child could feel her mother's heart beating. In the midst of her blessedness she felt shy and awed. She submitted to the embrace without returning it, only looking up at her out of the depths of blissful, wondering eyes.

"And can you *really* stay with me?" she asked very gravely. "Has the visitor gone?"

"Oh, yes," answered the mother, and she bent her head to untie the ribbon of her little one's bedroom slipper.

There followed a silence while the lady folded back the silken cover of the bed and made all ready—a silence of reverie on the one hand, of ignorant, wondering sympathy on the other. It began to weigh upon the little heart.

"Well, mother darling," she ventured at last, with tentative tone and smile, "I s'pose—well, I s'pose you don't feel inclined to *tickle* me, or anything like that, do you?"

The quaint overture surprised the lady out of her reverie and made her smile. "I think I feel inclined to do anything you ask of me," she said, lifting her little girl on to the bed.

Aurelia was immediately at ease with her mother again. "Hurrah!" she cried, bouncing up and down on the bed. "Hurrah! Hurrah! Hurrah! D'you really mean it, dearest?" She put her head on one side, and wheedled. "I s'pose you couldn't let me have Bluebell to sleep with as well as you? I don't s'pose you *could* do that, *could* you now?"

Bluebell—"my night-toy," as she described the huge toy rabbit, with shoe-button eyes, which had lain in her arms so many nights that all his protuberances were worn bald and shiny—had always been forbidden her mother's chamber and, as Aurelia firmly believed, had taken the slight to heart. Now for the first time he was to have an invitation.

"Hurrah! you *ex*quisite mother!" cried Aurelia, bouncing harder than ever; "and will you go on telling me the story, too? and will you go to bed now, when I do? and anything else I like? Now, whatever else *do* I like, I wonder?" she added anxiously.

"Well," said her mother, beginning to undo Aurelia's dressing-gown, "if we were in the middle of a story we had better finish it, I think. I'm very stupid to-night—what was it all about? and where did we get to in it? "

"Don't you 'member?" said Aurelia, and in her eagerness she hardly knew that the fluffy garment was taken off and she herself laid down and covered up in the luxurious bed: "it was about the Good Fairy who helped the Princess to be good, and the bad one who made her bad, and you didn't know which was going to win. Don't you 'member? Which *did* win, I wonder?"

"Yes, I remember now," the mother said.

She bent down and laid her head on the pillow beside the child, and looked and looked into those clear eyes—then she closed her own to hide her tears.

"Well, which *did* win, then?" asked the child.

"I think perhaps the Good Fairy—no, I'm quite *certain* the Good Fairy won the day," answered the mother.

THE PICTURES

JANET FRAME

She took her little girl to the pictures, she dressed her in a red pixie-cap and a woolly grey coat, and then she put on her own black coat that it was so hard to get the fluff off, and they got a number four tram to the pictures.

They stood outside the theatre, the woman in the black coat and the little girl in the red pixie-cap and they looked at the advertisements.

It was a wonderful picture. It was the greatest love story ever told. It was Life and Love and Laughter, and Tenderness and Tears.

They walked into the vestibule and over to the box where the ticket-girl waited.

One and a half in the stalls, please, said the woman.

The ticket girl reached up to the hanging roll of blue tickets and pulled off one and a half, and then looked in the money-box for sixpence change.

Thank you said the woman in the black coat.

And very soon they were sitting in the dark of the theatre, with people all around them, and they could hear the sound of lollies being unwrapped and papers being screwed up, and people half-standing in their seats for other people to pass them, and voices saying can you see are you quite sure.

And then the lights went down further and they stood up for God Save the King. The woman would have liked to sing it, she would have liked to be singing instead of being quiet and just watching the screen with the photo of the King's face and the Union Jack waving through his face.

She had been in a concert once and sung God Save the King and How'd you like to be a baby girl. She had worn a long white nightie that Auntie Kit had run up for her on the machine, and she carried a lighted candle in her hand. Mother and father were in the audience, and although she had been told not to look, she couldn't help seeing mother and father.

But she didn't sing this time. And soon everybody was sitting down and getting comfortable and the Pictures had begun.

The lion growling and then looking over his left shoulder, the kangaroo leaping from a height. That was Australian. The man winding the camera after it was all over, The Eyes and Ears of the World, The End.

There was a cartoon, too about a cat and a mouse. The little girl laughed. She clapped her hands and giggled and the woman laughed with her. They were the happiest people in the world. They were at the pictures seeing a mouse being shot out of a cannon by a cat, away up in the sky the mouse went and then landed whizz-thump behind the cat. And then it was the cat's turn to be shot into the sky whizz-thump and down again.

It was certainly a good picture. Everybody was laughing, and the children down the front were clapping their hands.

There was a fat man quite close to the woman and the little girl. The fat man was laughing haw-haw-haw.

And when the end came and the cat and mouse were both sitting on a cloud, and the lights were turned up for Interval, and the lolly and ice-cream boys were walking up to the front of the theatre, ready to be signalled to, well then they were all wiping their eyes and saying how funny how funny.

The woman and the little girl had sixpence worth of paper lollies to eat then. There were pretty colours on the screen, and pictures of how you ought to furnish your home and where to spend your winter holiday, and the best salon to have your hair curled at, and the clothes you ought to wear if you were a discriminating woman, everything was planned for you.

The woman leaned back in her seat and sighed a long sigh.

She remembered that it was such a nice day outside with all the spring flowers coming into the shops, and the blue sky over the city, Spring was the nicest of all. And in the boarding-house where the woman and little girl lived there was a daffodil in the window-box.

It was awful living alone with the little girl in a boarding-house.

But there was the daffodil in the window-box, and there were the pictures to go to with the little girl.

And now the pictures had started again. It was the big picture, Errol Flynn and Olivia de Havilland.

Seven thousand feet, the woman said to herself. She liked to remember the length of the picture, it was something to be sure of.

She knew she could see the greatest love story in the world till after four o'clock. It was nice to come to the pictures like that and know how long the story would last.

And to know that in the end he would take her out in the moonlight and a band would play and he would kiss her and everything would be all right again.

So it didn't really matter if he left her, no it didn't matter a bit, even if she cried and then went into a convent and scrubbed stone cells all day and nearly all night. ...

It was sad here. Some of the people took out their handkerchiefs and sniffed in them. And the woman in the black coat hoped it wasn't too near the end for the lights to go up and everybody to see.

But it was all right again because she escaped from the convent and he was waiting for her in the shelter of the trees and they crossed the border into France.

Everything is so exciting and nice thought the woman with the little girl. She wanted the story to last for ever.

And it was the most wonderful love story in the world. You could tell that. He kissed her so many times. He called her beloved and angel, and he said he would lay down his life for her, and in the end they kissed again, and they sailed on the lake, the beautiful lake with the foreign name. It was midnight and in the background you could see their home that had a white telephone in every room, and ferns in pots and marble pillars against the sky, it was lovely.

And on the lake there was music playing, and moonlight, and the water lapping very softly.

It is a wonderful ending, thought the woman. The full moon up there and the lights and the music, it is a wonderful ending.

So the woman and the little girl got up from their seats because they knew it was the end, and they walked into the vestibule, and they blinked their eyes in the hard yellow daylight. There was a big crowd. Some had shiny noses where the tears had rolled.

The woman looked again at the advertisement. The world's greatest love story. Love and Laughter. Tenderness and Tears. It's true, thought the woman, with a happy feeling of remembering.

Together they walked to the tram-stop, the little girl in the red pixie-cap and the woman in the black coat. They stood waiting for a number three car. They would be home just in time for tea at the boarding-house. There were lots of other people waiting for a number three car. Some had gone to the pictures too, and they were talking about it, I liked the bit where he, where she.

And although it was long after four o'clock the sun seemed still to be shining hard and bright. The light from it was clean and yellow and warm. The woman looked about her at the sun and the people and the tram-cars, and the sun, the sun sending a warm glow over everything.

There was a little pomeranian being taken along on a lead, and a man with a bunch of spring flowers done up in pink paper from the Floriana at the corner, and an old man standing smoking a pipe and a school-boy yelling Sta-a-r, Sta-a-r.

The world was full of people and little dogs and sun.

The woman stood looking, and thinking about going for tea, and the landlady saying, with one hand resting on the table and the other over her face Bless those in need and feed the hungry, and the fat boarder with his soup-spoon half-way up to his mouth, The Government will go out, and the other boarder who was a tram-conductor answering as he reached for the bread, The Government will stay in. And the woman thought of going up stairs and putting the little girl to bed and then touching and looking at the daffodil in the window-box, it was a lovely daffodil. And looking about her and thinking the woman felt sad.

But the little girl in the pixie-cap didn't feel sad, she was eating a paper lolly, it was greeny-blue and it tasted like peppermints.

The Silver Cloak

Winifred Holtby

Annie Moorcroft took the pins out of her mouth, began to say something, thought better of it, and put them in again. For Miss Adela was gazing at herself in the long mirror with melancholy resignation, and Annie felt that to say what she thought about the fit of the cloak and tunic would be a piece of needless cruelty.

"I'm sure, Miss Adela, there must be a way," she said at last, but she said it doubtfully.

Annie was an artist. She was also an optimist, harbouring a pleasant delusion that for most of life's problems there must be "a way." Even now, after snipping, pinning and tacking at the garment which Miss Adela had so rashly bought ready-made in London, she hated to confess to herself that she was beaten. She had been the village dressmaker at Kepplethorpe for fifteen years, and if that experience could not give her a mastery over obstinate figures and unadaptable styles, nothing could have done it. She sat back on her heels, puckering her smooth forehead.

"Well, I'm sure, Miss Adela, I hardly know what to say. It's a lovely material too. Hand-knit every stitch, I'll be bound. Just like a bit of silver."

"I know it's lovely material. And it cost ten guineas. And I look a perfect freak in it. Let's take it off."

The squire's daughter sighed. She did not like being fat, and she did not like wasting money, and she did not like the knowledge that if it had been Annie who was trying on the cloak, the fitting would have been a different matter.

Yet as she looked down at the supple slenderness and fresh vitality of the dressmaker, she felt no envy, only a half-comical regret. Annie Moorcroft was three or four years older than she was, and she looked like a girl. At twenty-six she had been the prettiest creature in the East Riding. At thirty-six her only serious rival was her daughter, a tall young woman training to be a teacher, as fair and dimpled and golden as her mother was brown and vivacious and petite. Katie was like the father, Ted Moorcroft, foreman to the joiner in the village, and himself a fine fellow, who had won the hurdles and obstacle race for three years running in the Club East Sports.

Miss Adela slowly pulled off the cloak and tunic, then suddenly her face brightened.

"Annie, I've got an idea. Just slip it on yourself, will you? I want to see how they really ought to hang. The tunic and cloak, I mean. Do you mind?"

Mind? Annie's fingers had been itching to handle the lovely material. Her eyes were hungry to see the long tunic, like fine mail armour, on her boyish figure. She knew how her flower-like throat must rise from the dull, gleaming silver, and how the cloak would swing gallantly from her slender shoulders. It was made for her. But she blushed with guilty pleasure as she dressed herself in the lovely garments and turned with half shy, half daring amusement to the younger woman.

Miss Adela was generous.

"Well, of course, my dear. You look too perfectly marvellous. It's simply your garment. It's heaven sent. You look like Joan of Arc and thingumebob and all the rest of it. You'll turn everybody's head if you come to church like that next Sunday. You've simply got to keep it."

"Oh, I couldn't. I couldn't do that."

"Of course you must. It's the perfect solution. You'll save me from the trouble of giving it away to a cousin or something, who'll hate me for patronising her, and you'll remove the temptation of my making a fool of myself by trying to wear it. And I shall have the pleasure of seeing something really nice for my money. Go on, Annie. Don't be a donkey. I shall be hurt if you won't take it."

"Well, I'm sure, I don't know. It's very kind of you."

Annie looked at Miss Adela, plump, voluble, excited, in her grey petticoat. She looked at the dignified, exquisite little figure in the glass, at her rumpled brown hair, at her glowing cheeks and the rich folds of heavy silk, and again she frowned in hesitation. For she did not take things from her customers. Ted would not like it. It wasn't as if he did not earn good money, nor as if her own clothes were not the envy of most other young women round Kepplethorpe, though she did make them all herself. And Katie would soon be earning too, once she had finished her training, and really become a teacher.

Annie had a notion that Katie did not want to teach all that much. She wanted to settle down and marry and have a nice home. Of course she did, dear, big, funny Katie. Annie smiled a little secret smile, which woke the dimple lurking near her red, curving upper lip. She was thinking what a clever mother-in-law she would be, and what fun it was to make young men hang about the house who thought that they came to see her and were really destined for Katie. She would try them all out. Her daughter should have the whole neighbourhood to choose from. Even though she was only the child of a joiner and a dressmaker, Katie should have no call to be ashamed of her parents.

After all, the silver cloak might be just part of the whole business. It wasn't an ordinary cast-off.

"Well, I'm sure, Miss Adela, if you really don't want it."

The bargain was made. Annie left the Hall with a neat brown paper parcel under her arm.

She set off home between the flowering hawthorn bushes and the road, her feet almost dancing along the soft, springing turf. For it was fun to be alive, and to be young and pretty. It was fun to know that in all Kepplethorpe nobody had a neater ankle and a prettier face. It was fun to know that Ted was real soppy about her after nineteen years of married life, and that Katie was coming home for next week-end, and they would all go in to Hardrascliffe together for Saturday afternoon. It was fun to know that she would wear the silver cloak.

She wouldn't say anything to Katie and Ted about it. It would be a surprise for them. When she had washed up the dinner things on Saturday, she would run upstairs and change and then call to Katie. Katie loved to see her looking nice. She felt sorry for mothers who were so much older than their daughters that they couldn't share all the jolly things like clothes and parties and dancing. That was the best of marrying at eighteen. You stayed friends with your daughter. Like sisters, they were, she and Katie, although Kate was so much better educated. It never seemed to matter. After all, it was because she had worked all these years that Katie could go to the High School and the Training College. Proud. They were each proud of the other and Ted was proud of them both. It was the nicest kind of family. All friends. All young.

She wanted to sing and to dance and to hold her arms to the bright spring sunlight. She hardly heard the sound of a motor-car snorting spasmodically in the road behind her, until a young voice called, "Hullo, Mrs. Moorcroft!"

"Hullo! Why it's Tom! My word, you are a stranger! And to think that we'd been harbouring an angel in our midst all the time, and never knew it till you took that solo in church on

Sunday. Well, it was a treat and no mistake. When did you learn to sing, eh?"

"Well, I'm sure you're very kind. Awful ass I felt. Won't you have a lift? If you don't mind the old bus."

Tom Barrow was a young farmer, one of the several possible suitors for Katie. Good position, too, and a good steady fellow. It was, of course, not quite usual for a farmer to marry a joiner's daughter. But then ... Annie climbed into the car, and made a little grimace at the dusty seat. Tom wiped it for her with his handkerchief, and settled her in, as she sat with her neat little shoes together on the rattling footboard. All the way back to the Moorcrofts' cottage they got on exceedingly well, and Tom quite forgot his timidity, and finally offered to drive their family party into Hardrascliffe next Saturday.

Bubbling with amusement and self-satisfaction, Annie said good-bye to him, and let herself into her front parlour with the dimple playing in and out of her cheeks. She really was a model mother-in-law.

She felt more pleased about the silver cloak than ever.

The day came warm and sunny, exactly as she had wished. When Katie arrived and called to her mother, Annie answered from the bedroom.

"Come upstairs, darling. I've got something to show you."

Annie turned from her dressing-table in the small cottage room to face her daughter. About her shoulders swung the silver cloak. Her brown hair was covered by a close-fitting blue hat. Her slim legs gleamed in pale grey stockings. Her eyes danced with glee.

"Oh, Katie, what d'you think? Do you like it? Oh, do you like it? I could hardly bear to wait to see you! Miss Adela gave me it because it don't fit. Come and give your mother a kiss and tell her she looks marvellous. That's what Miss Adela called me. Marvellous. Come and tell your marvellous mother what you think of her!"

She shrugged her shoulders so that the cloak swung from side to side. She stretched out her arms and kissed her daughter. She glanced backward into the looking-glass. She said, "Do you think Ted will like it?" She said, "Did you get here quite easily?" She said, "Did you know that Tom Barrow was going to drive us into Hardrascliffe in his car?"

To all of which the girl answered by a slow, deep blush, and a dragging sentence, "It's very nice, Mother."

"Very nice? I should think it is very nice. It cost ten guineas, no less. And I'm thirty-six, my love, though you mightn't think it. Now let's look at you. Yes. That blue does suit you, doesn't it? I'm glad I made you have the skirt altered. My goodness, that smocking took a time, I can tell you."

But Katie did not respond as usual to her quick, eager voice. Annie's laughing words tossed and broke themselves against her bleak indifference. Yet she handled the knitted silk, and looked and looked at her mother, as though she could never tire of watching the sunlight gleaming in the hanging folds.

"You said Tom Barrow was coming?" she asked at length.

"Yes. I met him on Wednesday. He gave me a lift back from the Hall. You should have heard him sing in church last Sunday. I did chaff him." She smiled impishly, coquetting with her tall daughter; but her mind was not quite easy. Something was wrong with Katie. She was more silent than usual. Not jolly somehow.

"Tired, dear?"

"No, thank you."

"I wish I had a long glass. When you get your first term's salary you can just buy me one, young woman. Look here, Kate. I wish you'd slip it on yourself. I want to see if the cloak covers the edge of the tunic. It'll be too short for you, you great creature. But I'll get some idea of the hang. I had to alter it a bit."

"There's not time, Mother."

"Oh, yes, there is. There's half an hour. It's your colour too. Don't be a silly."

Slowly the girl yielded, pulling off her own blue serge and putting on the shining garments. Then she too looked at herself in the glass and the deep blushes flooded her round cheeks again.

Why, it was her dress. The silver sheen just suited her fair hair and her blue eyes. The hanging cloak was kind to the angularity of youth. It gave her the dignity which she lacked, making her look no longer coltish, but tall and regal and almost what you might call noble. Katie knew very well that it suited her.

"Yes. I thought it would suit you. Now turn to the left a bit. Keep still."

Annie's voice sounded with a new note of hardness. Why, this was her dress. Miss Adela had given it to her. Why should Katie come and make her feel mean about something which was her own? She had made Katie that blue frock. She had made all her dresses for the Training College, sitting up night after night after her own work was finished. Katie couldn't expect everything.

"That'll do. Take it off," she said shortly.

"It suits me," mumbled the girl. "It's a town dress, really, isn't it? Not a country dress."

So that was it. Katie wanted it for herself. Well, then, she must learn not to be selfish.

"I've spoiled her," thought Annie. "I've always given her what she wanted. I've made a sister of her. But she mustn't take advantage of it. Girls are like that nowadays. Greedy. They want all the fun."

"Hurry up. We'll be late. Why, there's Tom coming up the road." She leant out of the window, waving a bare rosy arm.

"Tom, Tom! We'll be down in a minute. Come in and talk to Ted."

"I don't think I'm coming," said Katie. "I've got a headache."

Annie stared at her. Perhaps that was it. Perhaps she really had a headache, and that was why she seemed so queer.

"Have they been overworking you? You've been sitting up to all hours with those books, I expect?"

She wanted to go. She had been looking forward so much to this day at the seaside, having a good time, and riding in Tom Barrow's motor-car instead of in the village bus. How tiresome of Katie.

"Why not have a cup of tea? That'll set you up?"

"I don't want to go," repeated the girl obstinately, her pretty mouth set in a sullen line. "You go. Don't take any notice of me. You'll look fine. Here, put on the cloak quick and go down to them. Don't keep them waiting."

"Why, Katie. What's the matter?" Annie's golden day fell splintered about her feet. She felt a hot anger against Katie, and against the contrariness of things. She wanted her good time. She had worked so hard all the week. She wanted to show herself off in the silver cloak, and to be admired, and to have Ted walking round and round her growling funny little comments of admiration. She wanted to watch Tom Barrow blushing as she teased him. It was too bad of Katie.

"Oh, well, if you're really ill, of course I can't go. I can tell Tom we're not going." She looked round for her old dress to wear it when she went to deliver her message.

"Oh, you go. Don't take any notice of me. They won't want me. Tom Barrow hasn't eyes for any one but you. You wear your pretty new clothes. I'm sure I shall be all right till you come back. I'll just lie down a bit. He won't even know I'm not there when he sets eyes on you, I'm sure. I don't want to hang about all day just listening to you and him paying compliments."

"Why, Katie?"

Annie stared at her daughter, and as she looked, the hot shame brought dark blushes to her own cheeks, bathing her neck in warm colour. "Why, Katie!" Katie was jealous. Jealous of her. She had been a thief. She had wanted to steal the pretty things and the attention and the fun which belonged to youth by right of birth. She had been greedy, usurping the girl's place, because, through her own experience, she knew so much better than Katie what to say and do and wear. She saw the lovely relationship which had bound them so closely breaking down before her grasping desire for a good time. And all for a cloak, a silly silver cloak which wasn't even very suitable.

Why, she was an artist. She knew what was right. She knew that a village dressmaker of nearly forty—well, she *was* nearly forty, anyway—can't wear the same sort of things that a pretty young teacher can wear. She knew that it was time for her to step aside and yield the centre of the stage to her daughter. The game which she had been playing was very pleasant, but it wasn't right somehow any longer.

She gave a little gasp.

"Why, Katie, you goose! You didn't half fall for it, did you? Of course I meant them for you all the time. An old hag like me? What do you think I made you put them on for? Come on, darling. Tom's all eyes for you. I'll make you a cup of tea for your poor head. Ted and me's going to sit at the back of the car and enjoy ourselves this afternoon, so don't you go intruding on us, you young people."

She snatched up her last summer's coat and skirt, her fingers trembling on the buttons. She laughed at her daughter through eyes tempestuously bright. She ran downstairs to put on the kettle, and then out into the garden. She did not know why her breath came in quick, gasping sobs. She did not know why, as she crouched among the gooseberry bushes, the tears pricked her eyelids. But when she had pulled herself together and returned to the cottage, she found Katie in the sitting-room, all radiant and blushing, turning slowly round for the entranced inspection of her father and Tom Barrow.

They hardly noticed Annie when she came into the room, and Tom Barrow never even said "How do you do!" to her until she cried, "Oh, Katie, you might just run upstairs and see if I closed the window. Your legs are younger than mine, my dear."

And to the bewildered Tom she said with ravishing sweetness, "You know, my rheumatism has been so bad lately. When you get middle-aged, you do like a daughter to run about after you"—she twinkled—"or a son."

History Again Repeats Itself

E. M. Delafield

Theodosia was a very modern girl. So really, thoroughly modern, that it wasn't in the least necessary for her to talk about it, in the way that modern girls of more than twenty-five years old sometimes had to talk about it, in order to make perfectly certain that they weren't mistaken for the pre-war generation of girls. Theodosia, at the date of the Armistice, had been exactly nine years old.

She knew nothing about the Great War, except that middle-aged people could be very boring about it, and she thought that any allusion to it was in bad taste.

Although Theodosia was so modern, and an advocate of Communism, Legalized Polygamy, Birth-Control, and many other reforms, she had rather strict views about the privileges that should, and those, more particularly, that should not, be conceded to old people. With her own father and mother, she often found it necessary to be quite definite. Her father was at the rather difficult age of forty-nine—old, to all intents and purposes, and yet sufficiently active (especially at tennis, which he played remarkably well) to look upon himself as only middle-aged—and her mother at the still more difficult age of a young-looking forty-three.

Theodosia was far too modern to dislike her parents, or to feel rebellious in their regard. There had, indeed, never been anything for her to rebel against. And the parents did not rebel, because they admired Theodosia, and had been accustomed to her beneficent rule for nearly twenty years.

She was quite willing to live with them, and remained at home whenever she was not paying visits, or spending a week at her club in London. When she was at home, she almost always had a friend staying with her.

Most of Theodosia's friends were young men. Her father and mother quite understood that nowadays girls didn't flirt, or have love-affairs. They just had pals. And so even Theodosia's mother—who could easily have been a sentimentalist, but for Theodosia's bright, kind repressions of her—appeared to take Alec Forrest quite for granted. That was a relief, sometimes, for Theodosia, because occasionally she found herself wondering whether one day, in a very distant future, she might not marry Alec. And if her parents had wondered the same thing, it would have made it altogether obvious and impossible.

Alec was twenty-five. He worked in the firm of his very rich father, and worked hard. His father had made him begin at the very bottom. It had, however, been possible for him to move steadily upwards from the very bottom with a rapidity unknown to hard workers who are not the only sons of very rich fathers. He shared a flat in London with two other men, and he had a powerful, steel-coloured car with disc wheels, and a ukelele.

In person Alec was tall, good-looking in the prevalent style of 1929, and always clad in the very latest fashion for young men. He had of course written a book, and was preparing a collection of his letters for publication, written to a friend during his schooldays. To

Theodosia, he admitted that the friend was imaginary. He was very frank with Theodosia, and she with him. They had danced together whenever Theodosia was in London, or Alec staying at her home in Buckinghamshire, every evening for nearly a year, and they had gone out together in Alec's steel-coloured car, and in Theodosia's Morris-Cowley two-seater, and they had had cocktails and cigarettes in the lounge of the Regent Palace Hotel together, and in a great many other places as well, and, above all, they had talked and talked and talked together.

Theodosia had psycho-analyzed Alec, and Alec in return had psycho-analyzed Theodosia, and each had psycho-analyzed him or her self in the presence of the other.

Almost the only thing that Alec had never done, was to make love to Theodosia.

There were, of course, plenty of other men to do that, but Theodosia and Alec, dissecting Theodosia, had decided that she was almost a purely mental type, and not at all temperamental. So Theodosia very candidly told the men who, as occasionally occurred at dances, tried to kiss her, that she happened to be terribly highly evolved, and that it wasn't any use. They might, if they wanted to, of course, only they mustn't expect Theodosia to be anything but bored.

After that, they hardly ever did want to any more, but Theodosia danced so beautifully, and was so entirely unruffled about it all, that they still went on dancing with her.

Mrs. Renton, the mother of Theodosia, was very proud of her daughter's dancing. Really foolish about it, Theodosia considered, because, after all, it hadn't anything to do with her. It wasn't even inherited, since Nancy Renton wistfully admitted that she'd never been a good dancer. That was one reason why she had Theodosia taught dancing from the time she was four years old.

"I so well remember the humiliation of being a wall-flower. I often was, especially in my first season. I wasn't as pretty as you are, Theo."

"No one could have been pretty in the awful clothes you had to wear," returned Theodosia, who had seen, and shuddered at, photographs of her mother in a very elaborate 1906 balldress and *coiffure*.

Theodosia, herself, dressed particularly well. Her skirts stopped short just below her knees, and her chest was as flat as a boy's, her Eton crop as close-cut. Her mother was quite mistaken in applying the word "pretty" to Theodosia. She was handsome, with large, alert, intelligent hazel eyes, a beautiful complexion, and perfect teeth. Her nose was straight, and her mouth rather large, but very well shaped. She usually wore small, felt hats crushed down over one eye, wool sweaters coming up to her chin in winter, and sleeveless silk frocks in summer. She spent more money upon her shoes and stockings than upon any other single item of her wardrobe. She always looked, what she always felt, thoroughly efficient. The only person who could ever make Theodosia feel less than thoroughly efficient was Alec Forrest, whose own efficiency was quite flawless.

However brilliant, daring, fearless, and cynical Theodosia might be in expressing herself—and she and Alec fully recognized that self-expression was the duty, as well as the pleasure, of all highly-evolved moderns—Alec was always even more brilliant, daring, fearless, and cynical than she.

He often stayed at Theodosia's home, Palincourt. The year that Theodosia was twenty, he came to them for Christmas.

"I'm afraid that father and mother are hopeless about Christmas," she warned him, with a smile. "They like to have children in the house, if possible, and Christmas carols and presents, and mistletoe in the hall. In fact, they look upon the Christian festival as an excuse for giving the servants a great deal of extra work, and encouraging all their friends to eat too much."

"Will there be turkey and plum-pudding?" said Alec, slightly shuddering.

"There will. And mince-pies and crackers as well."

"And *church*?"

"For them, of course. Nobody else will be obliged to go."

Theodosia looked a little uncomfortable, but she was honest.

"As a matter of fact, I do go, at Christmas—just to please them."

"Isn't that rather feeble? I mean, it's sacrificing your individuality, isn't it?"

"Alec, I don't think so. They know it's a concession to their weakness. And there's never any question of my going at any other time. But there's something about Christmas—well, they've always enjoyed it so, poor dears, one can't grudge it to them."

Alec shook his head.

"I'm not going to say that it's very sweet of you, Theodosia, or anything like that. It's revolting sentimentality and weakness, that's all. Of course, don't interfere with their pleasure, but don't, for Heaven's sake, be a hypocrite. That's despicable!"

Naturally, Theodosia, who had often agreed with Alec that plain speaking, at all times and upon all subjects, was the essence of friendship, and that no person of candour and intelligence could ever be anything but grateful for the truth, was not hurt as anyone less modern might have been hurt by such fearless criticism. She certainly experienced a very strange and unpleasant sensation, partly physical and partly mental, that seemed to find its culminating points in her throat, behind her eyelids, and in the middle of her breast-bone. But she gave no sign of these phenomena, and indeed refused to recognize their existence even to herself.

"If you feel you can't bear it, Alec, don't come. I really hadn't realized that you've never been with us before, at Christmas time."

"Last Christmas, I hardly knew you," Alec pointed out. "We'd met at that studio rag of Marjorie Kane's, but it wasn't till February that we went to *The Beggar's Opera* together." It was from that night at *The Beggar's Opera* that their friendship really dated. Theodosia vividly remembered the eager delight of first talking with Alec, and discovering, pell-mell, in enchanted haste, the number of points upon which they were in complete sympathy.

Now, of course, the friendship was an old-established affair, and one couldn't expect to experience the first glamour again. Alec, of course, took Theodosia for granted, and that—she told herself—was exactly what she wished and expected. In fact, it was so obvious that she wondered how she had come to think about it at all.

At home, with a large party in the house, she wouldn't have so much time to devote to Alec Forrest. She wondered whether he would resent it.

Theodosia chose two new frocks for the Christmas house-party, with immense care. One was an afternoon frock of black taffeta, tightly swathed in gold round the hips, and with a square neck outlined with gold thread, and the other was a petunia-coloured velvet dance frock, with a short flounced skirt and a delightful travesty of Victorianism in the plain, tight-fitting corsage, cut very low.

"It's lovely, darling, but I think you show too much of your shoulders," said Mrs. Renton, quite unexpectedly.

Theodosia laughed indulgently. Criticism from her mother was so exceedingly rare, that she could quite afford to treat it as a joke, although she was slightly astonished by it.

"You know, Theo, I really think sometimes that you don't quite understand," Mrs. Renton continued, more and more surprisingly.

Theodosia laughed outright, at that. She really couldn't help it.

"Dear, do explain! What don't I quite understand? One of those mysterious laws of etiquette that burdened your poor little conscience in the old, bad days when people danced square dances because round ones were considered improper?"

Mrs. Renton did not respond to Theodosia's playfulness at all. She replied rather pettishly:

"Square dances had gone out some years before I began dancing at all."

"I dare say they had, mother, darling. But the principle remains the same. Which of your cherished conventions is my poor petunia frock going to outrage?"

"It's not that a bit, darling—indeed it's not. Of course I know I am conventional, and perhaps old-fashioned, but there are certain things that haven't got to do with conventions at all, only with human nature. And *they* don't alter."

"Bravo, mother! Do go on. Yes, really, I mean it. I want to get at what's in the back of your mind, and help you straighten it out. What is it?"

"I hardly know how to put it, Theodosia," her mother faltered. "But, darling, you really are very—very attractive and nice-looking, you know—and it simply isn't fair to—to men who may admire you, to dress as you do, and let them take you about, and say anything they like in front of you—and then to get cold and dignified and cutting, if they attempt to—to—well, to make love to you."

"Mother!"

"Darling, don't be angry with me, please."

"I'm not in the least angry. But I'm disgusted—really, mother, there's no other word for it. Apparently what you mean is that you hold such a low opinion of men, that you think they feel themselves unjustly treated if a woman allows herself, and them, ordinary social freedom, and then doesn't proceed to the further length of being kissed every time he and she are left alone together."

"Oh, don't! You make it sound so dreadfully coarse, and, indeed, I didn't mean anything in the least like that."

"Then what did you mean?" Theodosia enquired coldly.

But Mrs Renton was quite incapable of explaining what she did mean. She was terribly confused and incoherent, and could find no reply at all to Theodosia's frigid and dispassionate analysis of her parent's point of view, as prurient, reactionary, and essentially early-Victorian.

"As though," said Theodosia scornfully, "sex was the only factor that counted for anything, between men and women."

Theodosia's mother had become accustomed, in a way, to the word "sex," although she seldom used it herself, but in this connection it certainly upset her very much indeed.

"I never thought of such a thing. I—I haven't got a horrid mind, Theodosia."

But Theodosia explained, very dispassionately indeed, that this was just what her mother had got. Almost all the people of her generation had, only some of the others had outgrown it.

Mrs. Renton was left without any answer at all, and Theodosia hung up the petunia frock in her wardrobe, and reflected that Alec Forrest had once told her that she looked her very best in evening dress.

The house-party was not a very large one. There were a married cousin and her husband, two babies, and a middle-aged schoolmaster, who had been ordered an immediate holiday. It was Theodosia's father who had heard about him, discovered him to be an hotel acquaintance of some years earlier and made that an excuse for inviting him to Palincourt for a fortnight's rest. Theodosia had raised her eyebrows good-humouredly, at the idea of the Reverend William Milton, but after all, she told herself that Xmas was the time of year when her parents expected to enjoy themselves. And neither they, nor Mr. Milton, need interfere with her own friends.

Besides Alec Forrest, she had asked Marjorie Kane, the artist friend at whose studio they had first met, and a young man called Felton Fleet, who had written a great many plays, one of which had once been played at a suburban Repertory Theatre.

These last three arrived together on December 23.

"You're just in time for the Christmas carols," Theodosia

murmured mischievously. "The waits are sure to come to-night. And, Alec, we've got a parson staying in the house!"

"Rather interesting," commented Alec. "I haven't seen one at close quarters since I was at the 'Varsity."

"This is a very harmless specimen, and quite a good dancer. We'll dance to-night."

Alec and Marjorie responded with the catchword of the moment. They appeared to have started a chaffing argument in the train as to the applicability or otherwise of the adjective "magnetic" to Marjorie, and this they continued, with only the most cursory appeals to the others for a verdict to which, if it had been given, they would obviously have attached no weight at all. Theodosia remembered that she, herself, had often been utterly absorbed with other similar problems and had found it strange that other people, when they were present, neither cared to join in with vehemence, nor to listen appreciatively.

Alec and Marjorie, however, were not really very amusing and, besides, it might make Felton Fleet and Mr. Milton feel out of it. Theodosia talked to them all the evening.

She danced with them, too, after dinner, much oftener than with Alec, whom, indeed, she rather ignored.

He was not, she decided, in the mood in which she preferred him. Probably the conventional atmosphere of a Merry Christmas, diffused by Theodosia's parents, was on his nerves.

It was slightly on Theodosia's own nerves, too. At least, she was feeling rather on edge without quite knowing why. Her married cousin annoyed her, with her continual prattle about the children, and the children themselves were too noisy. Marjorie Kane was too noisy. (Theodosia hoped that she was not developing a noise-complex. If so, it was probably due to the strain of having to listen to those inharmoniously-rendered Christmas carols every year.)

Marjorie was about seven years older than Theodosia, although she certainly did not look it. She was very dark, and very vivacious, with black hair that fell into the confusion of bobbed curls usually only seen upon magazine-cover pictures, an impertinent nose, and a pair of lovely, long-lashed grey eyes that looked very dark, set in the colourless delicacy of her small, pointed face. She was not nearly as tall as Theodosia, and her extreme slightness made her look smaller than she really was, and also much younger. She talked a great deal, all that evening and all the next day—mostly to Alec Forrest. It seemed to Theodosia that Alec was doing more listening, and less talking, than he usually did. This, she thought, ought to settle once and for ever the question as to his manners which had occasionally been forced upon her by the old-fashioned strictures of her parents.

Though it was absurd to think about manners, nowadays. Theodosia's thoughts, however, were much less rational, controlled, and well-ordered than usual.

All day long, on Christmas Eve, she felt actually cross.

Noise, again.

Too much noise, altogether.

Even Theodosia's mother, at tea-time, began to talk a great deal too much, as though to distract attention—Heaven alone knew whose—from something—Heaven alone knew what. It was impossible not to feel very impatient. The party wasn't being a success, Theodosia was convinced, and to a hostess that was disturbing. She helped to amuse her cousin's children after tea, and listened to their mother's tedious comments on everything that they said and did, and every now and then she threw a lively contribution of her own into the loud discussion raging between Alec, Marjorie and Felton Fleet as to the new divorce facilities.

General Renton had taken Mr. Milton off to the smoking-room, but presently the clergyman strolled back again into the hall. The children were sent up to bed, and Theodosia, feeling sure that the divorce argument would not amuse the clerical guest, sat down beside him and began to tell him why she did not approve of the Public School system.

She could not help hoping that Alec realized the sense of courtesy that caused her to devote herself to the superfluous visitor, and when Mr. Milton, in a quiet, agreeable, but slightly pedantic manner, began to answer her, she was thinking so much of what Alec might be thinking that she quite forgot to refute him. He did not, however, seem to notice it. Perhaps, reflected Theodosia, as the dressing-gong sounded and she stood up, clergymen were accustomed to having the last word.

She looked up at Mr. Milton, who was very tall, and as he smiled down at her, she observed, a trifle absent-mindedly, that he had a very nice face. Obviously, he was nearer forty than thirty, but in his youth he must have been a good-looking man, she thought.

It seemed quite a pity that he should be a parson and a schoolmaster.

Theodosia waited a moment for Marjorie, at the foot of the stairs, but Marjorie did not stir. She and Alec went on talking. It was Felton Fleet who rose, and Theodosia's mother. Theodosia, carefully adjusting her Eton crop before her looking-glass, heard Marjorie flying along the passage just twenty minutes later, and then Alec humming to himself as he came up the stairs.

Theodosia, who had meant to wear a black lace dress, suddenly changed her mind, and put on the new petunia velvet frock.

She decided that after dinner they should dance. Theodosia danced remarkably well.

So did Alec Forrest.

So, also, did Marjorie Kane.

This, Theodosia had perhaps not altogether realized, until she stood with Felton Fleet, watching Marjorie and Alec Charleston.

"How beautifully their steps go together," said Fleet.

"Yes, don't they? If Marjorie was just half an inch taller—"

"Oh, but men always prefer dancing with girls less tall than themselves," Felton Fleet ingenuously declared.

Theodosia, who stood five foot ten inches, laughed.

"Hark! Here are the carol-singers! We ought to stop the gramophone—oh, mother's doing it."

The dance-music ceased, and the sound of male and female voices singing in unison was faintly audible outside the window. A harmonium accompanied them. General Renton threw open the double doors of the hall. His guests gathered round, and some of them, at least, listened to the familiar strains of *Good King Wenceslas.*

Marjorie and Alec kept aloof, but although they still talked, it was in the lowest of murmurs.

Theodosia would have felt it to be against her musical principles, which were austere, actually to listen to *Good King Wenceslas* rendered, to the accompaniment of a harmonium, by the village choir—but she was not sorry to remain silent. She thought that perhaps she was rather tired.

After *Good King Wenceslas* came *Hark, the Herald Angels Sing!* Then Mrs. Renton spoke to the singers, and one of the servants brought a tray of coffee and sandwiches, and they were all invited into the hall.

Theodosia found herself helping Mr. Milton to hand round cups and plates. Her father and mother, and the two cousins, were talking to the singers, and Felton Fleet was standing by the table, looking rather shy, but interested. ... The other two were nowhere to be seen. Theodosia was not looking for them, but she was aware of this.

They did not appear until the carol-singers had concluded their evening's entertainment with *The Mistletoe Bough* and had all gone away again. Then Alec Forrest came and asked Theodosia to dance with him.

Marjorie danced with Mr. Milton, and Felton Fleet with Marjorie's married cousin.

Alec danced Theodosia out of the big hall, and into the empty library, where the electric light was still burning.

"I'm afraid I left it on," he said. "I retired in here while the rustics were warbling their lays."

"What were you and Marjorie talking about?" asked Theodosia lightly, very much engaged in plaiting the little tassel on a cushion. "I hadn't realized, by the way, that you two knew one another so well. I'm awfully glad I asked her here."

"Oh, but we don't!" Alec exclaimed. "Or at least we didn't, until yesterday. You know how sometimes one knows a person for months, just casually, without really finding them out—and then suddenly something seems to happen—and one discovers that there's something tremendously vital there—the sort of thing that makes a difference ever afterwards—" He stopped abruptly.

"Yes, rather," said Theodosia tonelessly.

"Marjorie's wonderful, really, isn't she?"

"Her work is very—"

"I don't mean her work—though, of course, it's first rate, and she's going to do something pretty big one of these days—but in herself. I've never met a girl as young as she is who understands Life as she does."

"You said that about me, when you first knew me," said Theodosia, far too quickly.

Alec stared at her.

"Your view of life," he said at last, "is quite different to hers. You're so—so academic, aren't you? Of course," he added hastily, "it's one of the things one admires so tremendously about you. But Marjorie—well, she's about the most stimulating, alive sort of person I've ever met."

In a flash of intuition, Theodosia suddenly understood that Alec, in the library whilst the carol singing was going on, had kissed

Marjorie. And it was Marjorie's reaction to the experiment that he characterized as her understanding of Life.

"You're in love with her," said Theodosia, before she could stop herself. Then she felt ashamed of her words. It was not that they struck her as being indiscreet—a word that had no place in the vocabulary of either Theodosia or Alec—but that so prompt a deduction might almost be open to the accusation of Victorian sex-obsession.

Alec, however, was not annoyed, although he did raise his eyebrows in apparent astonishment.

"Well, my dear," he said easily, "we can't all be as sexless as you are. I've always told you that you belong to the purely mental type. You're temperamentally frigid, without emotions."

"No, I'm not," said Theodosia crudely.

"You bet you are," said Alec, equally crudely.

They stared at one another.

A singular experience then befell Theodosia, and one that was entirely new to her.

She quite suddenly lost control of herself, and instead of speaking with her usual detached, analytical lucidity, she found herself uttering—in a very much raised voice—a series of impassioned assertions, many of which had not even the elementary merit of being true.

"I'm not frigid—it's all nonsense. It isn't that I care a damn what you think of Marjorie—or what she's like—or you think she's like. It's just that I can't bear to be so totally misunderstood. Just because I don't make myself cheap, you think—you say—not that it matters to me *what* you say, or that I'm in the very least bit annoyed—I'm only amused—it's laughable—" said Theodosia, and burst into tears.

She had never done such a thing since her twelfth birthday, and Alec himself could scarcely have been more surprised than was Theodosia. And at so utterly inopportune a moment, her mother came into the room.

Alec was standing, quite helpless, gazing at Theodosia, and Theodosia, her face blazing, had been compelled, by stark, unromantic necessity, to pull her handkerchief out from the top of her stocking. It was the sort of situation in which it is quite impossible, in real life, to disguise anything at all.

Nancy Renton caught her breath for a moment, and then she exclaimed:

"Theodosia, darling! I can see your toothache has come on again. This poor child, Alec, had a sleepless night, last night, with pain, but she wouldn't give in—"

"Mother! It's not—" Theodosia's voice broke down again.

"I can see she's awfully bad," exclaimed Alec. "You're on edge, Theodosia, and no wonder, if you've had a night with toothache—it's the most beastly thing in the world."

"Alec, I wish you'd go through into the hall, and get my bag. It's on the piano, and I've got some aspirin in it," said Mrs. Renton calmly.

Alec, with the utmost celerity, obeyed her.

"Mother, how dare you—what on earth do you imagine?" Theodosia chokingly began.

"Don't try to talk, darling," begged Mrs. Renton—and indeed to talk, when one is crying passionately and uncontrollably, is entirely disastrous, and very often quite impossible. It had become so now, in the case of Theodosia.

Being forced to recognize this, she sat violently down upon the sofa, which faced away from the door and held her handkerchief—which, surprisingly, was already soaked—to her face. She heard Alec's return, and her mother's calmly spoken thanks, and assurances that he could do nothing more, and had better return to the gramophone.

And then, after a moment, the door shut.

Theodosia waited until she felt that her voice was steady again, and then, rather tremulously, tried it.

"Mother, if you think that I need that sort of—of help, I can only say that you understand me even less than I thought you did."

No answer. But at least Theodosia had ascertained that her own powers of speech had returned.

"If you want to know, Alec and I had had a—a sort of quarrel, I suppose you'd call it—though it wasn't exactly that, because we've always understood one another perfectly—and please, anyway, don't think that I was cry—that I was upset because of anything to do with *him*—it wasn't—it was simply—"

Theodosia stopped, waiting for her mother to interrupt her and remove from her the onus of explaining away further the unexplainable.

Still the silence continued, and at last Theodosia, her eyelids smarting and her face burning, turned round.

The room was empty.

"More of mother's tact!" reflected Theodosia, with great bitterness, and wondered how in the world she was to get upstairs to her own room without passing through the hall where they were all dancing.

Then she noticed that the gramophone was no longer to be heard, nor the sound of voices from the hall.

Mrs. Renton must have shepherded them all into the billiard-room. It was impossible not to feel that that, at least, had been a good idea.

Theodosia, feeling oddly shaken, left the library. There was no one in the hall, but as she reached the top of the stairs, she met the Rev. William Milton.

It is well known that clergymen are accustomed to the sight of those in affliction, and Theodosia not unreasonably supposed that one of such a profession might be expected to display rather more, than less, tact than other people. Instead of which, Mr. Milton looked hard at her, looked again, and exclaimed in a tone of genuine dismay—

"Oh, my dear child! What is the matter?"

"Nothing," said Theodosia—amateurishly, as she herself felt.

"Nonsense. Can't I help—can't you tell me what it is?"

There was something soothing about his concern, after Alec's detachment and her mother's unprecedented, managing interference. Unfortunately nothing except Mrs. Renton's ridiculous explanation would come to Theodosia.

"It's a—a sort of toothache," she muttered.

Mr. Milton gazed at her, and his eyes smiled, though his mouth remained serious.

"Poor little girl," he said simply. "I know that sort of toothache. I've had it myself."

"Have you?" said Theodosia, and began weakly to cry again.

"It's very bad while it lasts, but it doesn't go on for ever, and sometimes it does help, a little, to tell someone about it. Couldn't you tell me?" said Mr. Milton gently.

"It's not very interesting—in fact, there isn't anything to tell."

"I think anything about you would be interesting," said the clergyman.

Such discernment was extraordinarily comforting, besides being very surprising.

"Come into the gallery," said Theodosia suddenly. "We can sit down there, and it's quiet. That is, if you really—"

"Of course," said Mr. Milton.

The carol-singers came to Palincourt again, on Boxing Night, and the house-party went into the hall to listen to them.

Theodosia saw Alec Forrest raise his eyebrows slightly at Marjorie Kane, and Marjorie shrug her shoulders all but imperceptibly in reply.

> "Good King Wenceslas went out
> On the feast of Stephen …"

came harmoniously from the darkness outside.

"My favourite carol," said Mr. Milton softly in Theodosia's ear.

"Mine too, I think," she murmured, critically.

Mothers and Daughters

Frances Gray Patton

The sisters, Emily Wade and Belle Honeycutt, were alone together in Emily's living room, for Henry Wade had retired to the library, where he was composing a speech to be made at a business convention, the little boys had gone to bed and young Laura Wade had stayed on at school for a ballet lesson and an early dinner meeting of a discussion group she belonged to. The room was adequately warmed by central heating, but the cold March rain rattling against the windows had a freezing sound, and the two women had drawn their chairs close to the pretty fire that burned, for the sake of ornamental effect, in the basket grate on the hearth. Until that day, they hadn't seen each other in more than a year, so they had been chatting with a spurious air of spontaneity—catching up on family deaths and operations and weddings in an effort to recover a sense of intimacy that they both regarded as a sort of blood obligation. But it was hard going. They had never been alike in temperament and they had lived apart, and quite differently, for a long time. Emily found it difficult to shake off the feeling that she had to keep up a front for Belle and conceal everything but the veneer of her life—harmonious, polished, uncomplicated—which she would show to a chance acquaintance. At last, however, she broached the subject that was constantly in her thoughts.

"I can't imagine why Laura isn't back," she murmured. "She said eight-thirty and it's a quarter to ten now."

"Don't fret," Belle said, "You know where she is. And she said that headmistress—that Miss Saint John you wrote me about—was taking all the girls home. What could be safer than to be chaperoned by a female apostle?"

"The name is pronounced 'Sinj'n,'" Emily said.

"Oh," said Belle. "Well, live and learn." A glint of amusement showed in her eyes. "You don't suspect the decorous Laura of slipping off to meet a sailor in a bar, do you?"

Emily tried to smile, but she considered her sister's jest coarse and not very funny. "Really, Belle!" she said. "But she might have telephoned. She knows I worry."

"*They* don't know anybody worries except themselves," Belle said. "And what do they worry about? How to wangle another cashmere sweater out of their threadbare parents."

"No. The child's not greedy," Emily said. But she hesitated, wondering if, after all, the child was greedy. Could that common, pathetic foible—the blatant desire to have more than one has a right to—lie at the bottom of Laura's incomprehensible moods, belligerent withdrawal of sympathy? Emily shook her head almost regretfully; that explanation was too simple. She gazed directly into Bell's small, country-shrewd eyes. "It's that she's so remote. So cold and hostile."

Those were strong words, and as soon as they'd left her mouth. Emily wished she could recall them. It was incredible that she should have spoken so to anyone, even a sister, of her own daughter. But curiously, she also experienced a sensation of relief, or at least of a fatuous anticipation of relief, like that of a woman who picks out a notably easygoing physician before whom to lay the symptoms of an obscure malaise that has frightened her, hoping not to hear her trouble diagnosed but merely to hear it dismissed—after some cursory questioning—as arising from a trifling disorder.

Belle reached out absently and took a chocolate from the box on the table beside her chair. She bit into it. "A marshmallow," she said. "Fate pursues me with marshmallows!" She laughed. She had the slow, creamy laugh of a woman without much malice or vanity—a woman whose heart has returned, after some aimless wandering, to the human animal's original longing for food and affability. Looking at her sister, Emily thought she did indeed bear a resemblance to the fat country doctor of their youth. She looked like Uncle Chad, who had practiced medicine for forty years, down in Georgia, by instinct and ear (for he'd seldom used the stethoscope that he wore around his neck), and without losing any more patients than the brisk, scientific men up here at the Hopkins. The likeness soothed Emily. It made her feel that she was back in the old office, where the air smelled of wintergreen and pipe tobacco and musty, leather bound books, and where the Hippocratic oath hung framed, above the shabby roll-top desk. In a minute, Uncle Chad would pat her hand and tell her she was as cute as a speckled pup and that all she needed was a spring tonic and maybe a few days of salt air at Sea Island.

"Laura didn't strike me as a monster when I saw her this morning," Belle said. "I thought she was real sweet to drive way down to the depot to meet an old aunt on a seven o'clock train."

"She's very fond of you," Emily said, feeling grateful for an opportunity to say something nice about Laura. "Frankly, I didn't want her to go. I thought the fog was too thick. But she insisted that she had to meet you because she couldn't be here for dinner …"

"It was a lovely gesture." Belle said. "It saved me a pretty penny, too. If I'd taken a taxi all across Baltimore …"

"Laura's always lovely to everybody except me," said Emily.

"Well, company manners are a useful thing to have," said Belle.

"It's not only company," Emily said "She makes a distinction right here in the bosom of the family. With the boys, she's the perfect big sister—always so kind and tolerant, you know—and you never saw such a dear little daughter as Henry has! Why, if *he* had asked her not to take the car out this morning, she'd have been perfectly reasonable about it, instead of putting up a fuss the way she did with me—telling me that I was neurotic and had no sense of responsibility toward a guest, and—"

"I'm sorry if I've been the cause of a row," Belle said.

"Oh, no." Emily assured her. "Not the cause. Only the excuse. She seems to like to find grudges against me."

Belle sighed. "I know!"

"And *only* me," Emily went on. "Now, last week she'd just recovered from the twenty-four hour flu and she was planning to spend the week end at Annapolis. One of her school friends has a brother there, and she and her mother had asked Laura to go down."

Belle nodded.

"I was prepared to let her go along," Emily said, "just to avoid unpleasantness. But Henry told her she ought to stay home and rest. She took it like a lamb from him. She called her friend and said her father thought she wasn't well enough for the trip, and then she went up to her room to read. Henry paced around looking like a man who'd lost his last nickel—he'd rather die than deny Laura any pleasure—and finally he got an apple and carried it up to her."

"An apple?" said Belle.

"Yes. Laura likes apples," Emily said. "So Henry found a big red one in the pantry and polished it all up and put it on a silver tray and—"

"What did Laura do?" Belle asked.

"I heard her exclaiming that he was just the sweetest most thoughtful daddy in the world," Emily replied. She laughed bitterly. "Now, if I had interfered with Laura's plans and then offered her an apple—"

"She'd have grabbed it and busted in your head with it," Belle said. Having consumed her marshmallow, she took the candy box onto her lap and began ferreting among its contents. "That's the way with girls," she said. "It's nature. I reckon the mother is a symbol of something they have to rebel against. Inhibitions or repressions or something." She selected an oblong chocolate-dipped candy and tested it gingerly between her front teeth. "A caramel," she grumbled, "and I was hunting for a Brazil nut! Listen. Emmy—didn't you ever hate Mama?"

"Why, no," Emily said. "I'm sure I didn't."

"I did," Belle said cheerfully. "Of course, I didn't call it hating, but that's what it was. Mama was so Christian and pure and understanding She took the edge off everything. Whenever I had any fun, like taking a drink of corn or going swimming at midnight with the Bellamy boys, I'd think how she'd trusted me. So I'd feel like a heel and hate her."

"She used to irritate me when I'd been to a party and she'd want me to 'tell all about it,'" Emily said, "but only because she was so eager. I don't remember her as a moral burden."

"You were the baby," Belle said. "Mama'd worn herself out on my character. Besides, you were always up in the clouds."

"What about your own children?" Emily asked.

"Oh, I don't know," Belle said. The shadow of some nameless emotion—resentment, disappointment, fatigue?—passed over her placid countenance. "But I don't feel about mine like you do about Laura. I never thought mine were found in the bulrushes."

That was a neat shot of Belle's, Emily admitted to herself. That was precisely how she, and Henry, too, had always regarded Laura—as a piece of good fortune, beyond their deserts, planted in their path by the miraculous grace of Providence. And within limits their attitude was defensible. Laura had indeed been a child to delight any parent. She had begun as an enviable baby, with dimples, coos and crows and all the other engaging attributes of infancy, and had grown into a fetching little girl who had possessed curly hair, a sunny disposition, an inquiring mind and the disarming manner of not acting as if she felt superior to other people. Without questioning the wisdom of their motives, the Wades had arranged the whole pattern of their life to revolve around their daughter. It was for her, really—in order that she could never reproach them with loneliness—that they'd decided to have the two younger children. It was for her—so that she could attend Green Valley Academy, the best and most expensive country day school in the vicinity—that Henry had worked hard and Emily had devised various tricks of juggling the household budget. It was for her that they had bought their modest but pleasant house in a neighborhood that was a shade more impressive, perhaps, than Henry's income warranted.

None of this had seemed to spoil Laura. She had done well at school and had made a number of close friends among girls from the elect of Baltimore society, but she had continued to be simple and unaffected. Nothing had appeared to please her more than to meet Emily in town for an afternoon concert and have a large tea, with sticky buns, and a long, friendly gossip afterward.

And then, last June, Emily had noticed a change. At first it had not been much. Laura had sulked for a few days when Emily had borne her off to the beach instead of permitting her to remain at home and find a summer job in a hospital or a department store. (Miss St. John, Laura had argued, had said you couldn't understand reality until you'd worked for wages.) After that, Laura had had, intermittently, periods of abstraction—of a kind of restless nervousness—when she seemed almost offended by her mother's conversational overtures and neglected, pointedly, to smile at family jokes. Emily had regarded Laura with sympathy. The child had been studying too hard, she'd thought, and now, with school closed and the tension removed, she was in a slump. Once she was rested, she would recover her old, accustomed equanimity.

But the summer ended and the fall and winter went by, and still

Laura was of uncertain temper. She was techy and gloomy by turns, and sometimes for a week at a stretch she would preserve a cool aloofness in the presence of her mother. On rare occasions, provoked by the merest trifles, she was openly insolent; she addressed to Emily cutting remarks couched in stilted language and assumed a la-di-da manner that would have been high comedy in someone else's daughter.

Emily tried to weather Laura's moods as best she could. They were a drag on her spirits, though. Several times, she considered appealing to Laura's sense of justice and affection—begging her to reveal whatever fancied injuries she nursed and to end the long, one-sided feud that she was waging. She never did, however, because each time she was on the verge of speaking, Laura's temper would clear as mysteriously as it had clouded. For a few days, she would be as responsive as she'd ever been. Emily thought these halcyon interludes too precious to be spoiled with upbraidings, and she had, moreover, an inkling that to remonstrate with Laura would be as fruitless as to urge an alcoholic to break the liquor habit; when he was drunk, he would be beyond the reach of reason, and when he was sober, he'd be unlikely to believe he could ever have been drunk.

So Emily suffered in silence. Not until this evening, when her sister's face made her think of the doctor she had loved, had she voiced her distress.

"My children—" Belle said in a musing tone. "Oh, the boys are all right. Wild. But boy's are expected to be wild in Georgia. Boys don't get under your skin like girls."

"No," Emily agreed. She thought of her sons, aged nine and eleven, who were asleep upstairs. She dwelt on them with tenderness, as if to make up for the fact that they didn't mean to her what Laura meant.

"But that Sally!" Belle continued. "She's peaches and pie now she's married and settled down—she knows I wouldn't baby sit for her if she wasn't! But when she was Laura's age she was mean as a snake. She was forever taking up with ratty people. She used to run around with the son of the biggest crook in Georgia—and you know we have some powerful big crooks down home! She drove over to Atlanta with him once when the legislature was in session and there were at least two people from every county in the state there to see her. They wandered up and down Peachtree Street holding hands and acting silly."

"Did you scold her?" Emily said.

"We had a disgraceful scene," Belle said. "Sally threw things and expressed indignation at my presuming to criticize her friends and her judgment. That was the sacred matter—her judgment! She called me names, and I climbed on my dignity and said if she didn't apologize, she'd have to stay in her room for three days." She shrugged. "It was a rash threat. I had company coming for over Sunday."

"What happened?"

"Oh, next morning I found a note under my door. It said, 'Mother, for the sake of peace and liberty I hereby apologize for calling you a bich'—she spelled it without a t—'and will you please call the cleaner about my green gabardine suit.'"

"What did you do?" Emily asked.

"I accepted the apology, though it still makes me mad to think of it," Belle replied. "I called the cleaner, too." She chewed hard on her caramel, half closing her eyes, as if to savor to the full the juice in her mouth and the juice of an imagined pleasure in her mind. "Suppose I'd ever called Mama a bitch!"

"The Lord would have struck you down," Emily said. "He was on the parents' side in our day."

"Yes," Belle said. "Remember those hand-painted mottoes people use to have in their parlors? 'God Could Not Be Everywhere, So He Gave Us Mothers!'"

Emily laughed, but she realized that the discussion had strayed afield from her own problem. "Laura isn't rowdy," she said. "I wouldn't have you think that, and, of course, she wouldn't be kept on at Green Valley if she were. She's seldom even downright rude."

"Well, then!" said Belle.

"It's something less tangible than that," Emily said. "And more painful." Her mouth felt dry, but she was wound up now and she went on talking, even though she was refining an already invisible point. "She holds me in contempt. She's shut me out of her life." She knew that her words sounded melodramatic, but she didn't care.

"It's that rich girls' school you send her to," Belle said. "All kids are snobs."

"No. Green Valley's not that kind of school," Emily said with conviction. "The pupils come from families that are sure enough of themselves to admire simplicity. And Miss St. John is a real aristocrat—plain as an old shoe. She believes in proper manners and solid scholarship and no nonsense."

"You sound like a brochure," Belle said.

Emily leaned toward her sister. "Oh, Belle," she said, almost in a whisper, "I've lost her! What am I going to do?"

Belle's plump face didn't show comprehension, but it showed compassion. "Don't let her get you down," she said. "I wanted to wring Sally's neck off. But I didn't let her get me down."

"Laura's different," Emily said.

"She's going through a phase. She can't help it any more than the moon can," Belle said indulgently. "And she doubtless has troubles of her own. Seventeen's a ghastly age." She popped a Jordan almond into her mouth. It rested in the pouch of her check and poked out, like a grotesque subcutaneous growth. "I wouldn't be seventeen again for the earth on a silver platter. Would you?"

Emily considered the question, "I don't know. Was it bad?"

"Your memory's failing you. It was miserable," Belle said. "Of course, I was the phlegmatic type. I just sweated through, bored to death. There was nothing to do, out there in the country, except go under the scuppernong arbor and eat grapes, or sit and help Mama make her mayonnaise. But you were artistic. You really suffered."

"Did I?" Emily said. She tried to visualize the scene of her old home. It seemed far away and rather wistful.

"Did you!" Belle exclaimed. "You wandered about like a lost soul. Everything hurt you. Especially beauty. There was a poem you composed on that theme:

> "'The beauty of this winy autumn day
> Is like a poisoned arrow in my breast. ...'"

"Stop!" Emily cried. "I never showed that to anybody!"

"No, but I used to read your things," Belle said calmly. "I thought that one was real sweet. Do you still write?"

"Heavens, no!" Emily said.

"You should. You had genuine talent," Belle said. "Me—I can't rhyme 'mine' with 'thine'! And then you were constantly falling in love with these impossible oafs who fell *out* of love before you did. It's a miracle you ever settled on a man as nice and normal as Henry."

"Were my beaux so strange?" Emily asked. She was fascinated in spite of herself.

"Well, there was that slue-footed instructor that you met—God alone knows how—when you were on a fraternity house party in Athens. He wrote you a scad of letters. Passionate, in a literary way. He called you 'dear heart,' and said you were a little willow tree trembling in the winds of dawn."

"You did considerable snooping in my desk," Emily observed dryly.

"I had to have *some* entertainment," Belle said. "And when he stopped writing, you went into a positive decline. You made a poem about that. It was good enough for the *Atlantic Monthly*. I memorized it."

"Just so you don't quote it," Emily said.

"But it was fine," Belle said. "It began:

> "'I lived before this love was born
> And I shall live long after,
> It lies beneath the verdant turf
> Of memories and laughter.'"

"I can't stand any more," Emily protested.

"The end was the strongest part," Belle said:

> "'I shall plant lilies on its grave,
> Whence perfumes rare shall start—
> But, oh, this cold, unburied thing
> Lies heavy on my heart!'"

Emily laughed aloud. "I was a genius, pure and simple."

"I showed it to Papa," Belle said. "He was planning to send you to Europe. To forget."

"I never knew that," said Emily.

"But then you got attached to the funny Bellamy boy—the one that chased butterflies."

"He's a distinguished entomologist now," Emily said stiffly.

"Good for him!" said Belle. "But he cost you a trip. Papa built himself a fish pond instead. Then there was—"

"Spare me the others," Emily said. "I was a child."

"You were seventeen," Belle reminded her. "Laura's age. Has it ever occurred to you that she might be in love?"

"Only in passing," Emily said. Swiftly she reviewed the half-dozen lads, with crew cuts and scrubbed faces, who had been underfoot during the Christmas holidays. "You see, the boys she knows are so young; most of them are in boarding school. And then, how could love turn her against me?"

"Everyone in love is crazy," Belle said.

"Oh, sure," said Emily. "But I don't think that's Laura's trouble."

There was a sound of someone coming in the front door. Emily turned in her chair. "Is that you, Laura?" she called.

"Yes, Mother," Laura replied from the hall. "Were you expecting Queen Elizabeth?" Her tone was civil but too overlaid with sarcasm to be entirely good-natured. "I'm hanging my coat in the storm closet. Now my hat. Now I'm taking off my rubbers!"

"She's trying to be clever," Belle said in a barely audible voice. "Maybe you are apt to ask her for a play-by-play account of herself. Don't let her rile you."

Laura came into the room. She was a slender girl dressed in the pastel-colored cashmere pullover (hers was blue) and flannel skirt that almost amounted to a uniform for her generation. Her complexion was naturally pale, but the night air had touched her cheeks with pink, and the ends of her soft, dark hair were lightly spangled with drops of moisture. Her general appearance gave the effect of the elegance and delicate vigor that are found in flowers of the field and gently nurtured daughters of the privileged American classes. She hurried, with a pretty air of pleasure, to Belle's side.

"Oh, Aunt Belle!" she cried in her properly modulated voice. "I feel as though I hadn't seen you at all. This morning didn't count I was in such a mad rush that—"

"You were a darling to meet me," Belle said. "I was telling your mother."

"I adore meeting trains," Laura said. "I feel so important. And then it was wonderful out this morning. I drove down Charles Street and saw the monument sort of looming through the mist, like the *idea* of a monument taking shape in a sculptor's mind!"

"How's the weather tonight?" Emily asked.

"The way it sounds," Laura said. She nodded toward a window and conveyed the impression that her mother had asked a stupid question. "Freezing rain." She sat cross-legged on the floor and looked up at Belle. "I'm sorry I'm late on your first evening," she said. "Miss St. John got talking and we lost track of time."

"What did you discuss?" Emily asked, wanting Laura to show Belle how intelligent she was.

"Gosh, I don't remember," Laura said coldly. "Just ideas." She turned to Belle. "I want to hear about Sally's baby. Imagine you a grandma!"

She stayed half an hour in the living room, turning on her charm like a lamp for Belle's benefit and dimming it perceptibly whenever she had to address her mother. "I suppose I must get to bed," she said at last, rising to her feet in a single movement. "It's hard to leave the fire and the special company." She bent and laid her cheek for an instant against her aunt's head. "Good night," she said. "I'll bring you a cup of coffee before I leave for school tomorrow. I remember you and early coffee! Good night, Mother."

"Good night, Laura," both women said.

They heard her stop and open the library door before she went upstairs. "Hi, Daddy," they heard her say, and her voice—though it was still Green Valley's best—was more artless than it had been in her conversation with Belle. "I just dropped by to peek at you. If you're driving me to school in the morning, I'd like to tell you about our meeting tonight. I got a lot of new slants on things and I want to discuss 'em with you."

Emily eyed her sister. "Well?" she said.

"I see what you mean," Belle said. "Of course, I'm captivated. She's so pretty and that thing about the monument in the sculptor's mind—it was sheer poetry! And what a vocabulary!"

"They stress vocabulary at her school," said Emily.

"And then I have an odd trick of liking anyone who's nice to me," Belle said. "But I see what you mean. She doesn't care for you very much at the moment. You'll have to trust to time." She smiled ruefully. "It's like Mama used to say when we were broken up about something that couldn't be helped. 'Don't struggle, lie down and let the waves beat over you.'"

Henry came striding in. He looked chipper, like a man who had been diverted by his own wit. "Have you girls mopped up the state of Georgia yet?" he asked. "How about a nightcap?" And to Belle, "Did you talk to Laura? She's my *chef-d'œuvre*."

Belle nodded. "You're very fortunate in your children. I like the boys, too."

"Oh, yes." Henry said carelessly. "They're splendid little chaps." He went out to the kitchen and returned with three strong-looking highballs on a tray.

"We ought to fix a little bar in the butler's pantry," Emily said idly.

"Or in your library, behind a sliding panel of false bookbindings," Belle said.

"We can wait until Laura's older and needs something more potent than Coca-Cola for her friends," Henry said. "Though that's a day I don't hanker for." He gave the ladies their glasses and raised his own. "To Demosthenes," he said. "The old gentleman led a hard life."

"How's your speech?" Belle asked.

"Adequate, I hope," Henry said, with a try at modesty. "It's a tough proposition, though. I want it to provoke thought but not slumber." He pulled a chair up close to Belle's. "I'm using one story you might appreciate, if Emily can stand it again."

Emily leaned back in her chair and sipped her highball. She hadn't had a drink for weeks (she was saving money for Laura's dancing lessons) and now she could feel the whisky taking hold almost as soon as she swallowed it. Before her glass was half emptied, her spirits began to rise on a wave of optimism and resolution. Now was the moment to be seized, she thought suddenly. Now was the time to have things out with Laura.

"Excuse me a minute," she said to Belle and Henry, who, engrossed in the swapping of anecdotes, gave no sign of hearing her. She went into the hall and up the stairs.

Laura's door was closed. Emily opened it quietly, without knocking. The room was dark except for a gentle, diffuse illumination that seeped through a window from a street lamp. Laura was not asleep. She was standing at the window, gazing out. She was wearing a white flannelette nightdress with long sleeves and a high neck, and her hair, drawn off her ears and brow, was pinned on top of her head. She had a look of timelessness—of unreality, even.

"Laura—" Emily said.

Laura turned. She had rubbed cold cream on her face and her skin glistened—not greasily, as middle-aged skin might hate done, but with a hard, high luster, like metal or ivory. "Is there something I can do for you, Mother?" she inquired.

"Yes," Emily said. "You can talk to me. You can tell me what's the matter."

"Nothing's the matter," said Laura. "Not with *me*. I was looking out the window. Is that a cause for alarm?"

"You know what I mean," Emily insisted. "You know how you've been acting to me."

"I haven't been acting any way," said Laura.

Emily sat down on the foot of the bed. "I thought we were so congenial," she said. "And then, last summer, something began to go wrong."

Laura was silent.

"What happened?" Emily asked. "If I've offended you, I think you should tell me how. In all fairness. What did I do?"

"Why did you make me go to the beach?" Laura asked.

"I thought you'd enjoy it," Emily said.

"Why did you think so?" Laura demanded. She spoke in a forced way, as if straining to revive an indignation she no longer really felt. "I told you I wanted to stay here and do something useful. But you just dismissed my preferences. You think you know all the answers, don't you?"

"Very few," Emily said.

"And tonight Miss St. John talked to us about values," Laura continued, sounding more confident now. "Perspective, and reality, and a sense of proportion, and how we took for granted luxuries that the mass of humanity would find incredible"

"Yes?" said Emily.

"And what did I find at home? You and Aunt Belle hovering over a fire you didn't need. Do you know how many families, right here in Baltimore, are actually cold?"

"How many?" Emily asked.

Laura hesitated. "A great many," she said.

Emily suppressed an unexpected impulse to laugh. "Oh, come on now, sweetie," she said. "You're trumping up grievances. You had a marvelous time at the beach. And you know Miss St. John wasn't hitting at people like us when she spoke of extravagance. She wouldn't begrudge me a fire in my sitting room."

"Well no, I guess she wouldn't," Laura admitted. "But you're so—" She stared through the shadows at her mother. Her eyes, catching the lamplight seemed to give off light of their own. "You have no depth."

"Don't I?" said Emily.

"I've felt it for a long time, and it hurts me," Laura said. "Miss St. John was reading us this thing in chapel the other day—this thing about passion. ..."

"Passion?" said Emily. She tried to imagine the head-mistress, a square-jawed spinster of fifty with a sea captain's voice, lecturing a hundred blossoming maidens on that tricky subject.

"Not the kind you mean. Not sex," Laura said severely. "A

dedicated passion for art and beauty. How you had to burn with a 'hard, gemlike flame.' It was a passage from Walter Pater. Did you ever read him?"

"A long time ago," said Emily. "Just a little of him."

"Well," said Laura, "you don't burn with his flame."

Emily shook her head regretfully. "I'm afraid I don't."

"You live on the surface," Laura told her. "Sunday afternoon I put Beethoven's Seventh on the record player, I nearly died, it was so tremendous. It was like great tides sweeping me away. And what did you do? You worked on a crossword puzzle."

"I was trying to remember the genus of 'goose,'" said Emily.

"You see!" said Laura. "As soon as the conversation gets meaningful you make a wisecrack. You retreat. Why, you haven't even noticed how beautiful the world is tonight." She took her mother by the arm and drew her to the window. "Look!"

Emily looked. Her house was on a hill, and across the road, where, the land began to fall away, stood an elm tree, large and symmetrical. Below the tree were rooftops of houses that seemed to form a flight of giant steps going down in the darkness. Tonight, in the ice storm, the elm was a great sequined fan and the ridgepoles were penciled silver lines.

"Doesn't it make you want to cry?" asked Laura.

"No," said Emily. She felt too tired and baffled for anything but the simple truth. "Not except when I think how slick the roads will be in the morning." She moved away.

"Oh, Mother!" Laura cried in a childish, urgent voice. The voice she used when she needed help.

Emily looked at her sharply. "Yes, Laura?" she said, forcing herself to sound casual.

Laura flung out her hands in a vague gesture of wonder and perplexity. She brought one of them to her breast. "Life is—" she said. Her voice broke.

"I know," Emily said gently. "But I must go back to Belle and Henry now. Get in bed soon, dear, and don't forget to shut the register before you open the window,"

When she returned to the living room, Emily found Belle there alone.

"Henry's gone to get me a dividend," Belle said. "La, Emmy! I'm in a golden haze!"

"Good," said Emily. "I must catch up with you." She sat down and took a swallow of her own neglected drink and thought of Laura. She smiled inwardly, recalling the high-flown phrases the girl had tossed about and the way she had rebuked her, Emily, for entertaining low associations with the word "passion." Then she thought of how Laura had laid her hand upon her heart, in a way that would have been trite on any stage in the world and that had seemed right and natural up there in the shadowy bedroom. And that pretty, unaffected gesture had evoked all the climate of youth. How would it be, she wondered, to stand again beneath a canopy of leaves, eating scuppernong grapes, warm off the vine, and feeling oneself the intimate and equal of beauty and love and pain? Or to look at an icy tree from a cozy room and speak of life?

"Well," she murmured to her sister, "it had its charms, no matter what you say."

"What had charms?" asked Belle.

"Being seventeen," said Emily.

Belle nodded. "It seemed dreadful when we were, but it was probably all right. We had so much time before us then, and we didn't dream it could ever run out." She put her hands to the fire as if to warm away a premonitory chill that had touched them. "You know, even mayonnaise doesn't taste the way it did."

Emily lowered her eyes to hide the amusement that she knew was in them. All roads of Belle's philosophy, she thought, led eventually to food.

"I think it's because we're always in a hurry," Belle went on. "We dump all the ingredients in together and turn on the electric mixer. Mama spared no pains with hers."

"It took hours," Emily said

"Yes," Belle said, "hours. On hot afternoons, she made it down at the springhouse, where she got the coolth of the valley air. You could hear the rain crows complaining in the grove." Her flat voice sounded drowsy and peaceful. "Mama saved the whites of the eggs for her angel cakes. She just used the yolks. I'd pour the olive oil for her, drop by drop, and she would beat it in with a silver fork."

The Shadow
of Kindness

Maeve Brennan

Mrs. Bagot missed the children. They had been gone twenty-four hours. It was exactly that length of time since she had put them on the train, in the care of the guard, and sent them off to her sister and brother in the country, where they were going to spend a month. She wished the month were over. She didn't know what to do with herself when they were away. Without them the house had neither substance nor meaning. The house was lonely, that is what it amounted to, and Mrs. Bagot felt the house was making her lonely. But the house was going to look very nice when the children came back. She was already planning what she would do to welcome them. She was going to put flowers all around—she would cut all the flowers in the garden. And she was going to bake a cake and put both their names on it in icing: "Lily," "Margaret." And then there were other things she was going to do, but these preparations, which she had already memorized and timed to the minute, still left her with nothing to do for a month but look *forward*, and she knew a grown woman should have more life of her own. Even if she had children, a woman should have a life of her own that would stand up when the children were out of the house for any length of time. She knew that. It was not right to let yourself get so lost in your children that you could find no trace of yourself when they were gone. What would she do when they grew up? Of course, it was silly to think of it; not silly—morbid. She was letting her imagination run away with her. She would make herself a cup of tea and cheer herself up. The tea would cheer her up. Still, she did not move. She continued to stand by the big window looking out into her garden.

The big window was the window in the dining room. It was very big, a sash window, and almost square, and at the moment it was very bare, because she had taken the curtains down for washing. The garden was almost out of sight behind the rain. The yellow rosebush seemed far away, a steady blur of brightness, like a street lamp in the fog. And the other flowers, not as intimately massed around one center as the roses were, and not so strongly defined, seemed to be moving about by themselves, swimming slowly about in the wet gray air and arranging themselves in different patterns from the ones she had imagined and seen come to life as the summer wore on. This was the heaviest rain they had had for a long time and she was glad to see it—it was needed. And she was glad it had come today and not yesterday. The children would not have liked traveling in the rain. They had been looking forward to the view from the train windows. And then there would have been all that worry about damp feet and damp heads. Yes, it was fortunate the rain had held off until now.

Earlier in the day, in the morning, when she saw the rain getting heavier, she went out and cut all the full-blown and half-blown roses. She cut the white, the pink, and the red—all but the yellow. The yellow rosebush had been in the garden when she and Martin moved here, and she had a particular affection for it, because she felt it had encouraged her to set to work and make the lovely garden she had out there now. She seldom cut a yellow rose, and this year, as they bloomed, the roses on that bush had arranged themselves so marvelously that it was as though a great artist had made them grow in that certain way to match a picture he had in his mind. And so this morning she had left all the yellow roses to survive or fall together. As well as she could see, they were holding up, in a round shape that tapered slightly toward the top—a dense, delicate ball of yellow that was like a Christmas tree ornament or an Oriental roof. It was accidental, that grouping. It might never occur again. She was glad she had not disturbed them.

The white roses, and all the pinks and all the reds, made quite a big bunch. She had put them around in this room and in the front room and in the hall, and then, foolishly, she had put a small bunch in the children's room to make it seem less deserted. When she wrote to Lily and Margaret tonight she would tell them there were flowers waiting for them in their room, beside their window, on the little table that was all marked and stained with chalk and ink and putty and plasticine. The window in the children's room corresponded with this window where she stood—they had the back bedroom. The paper on the walls of that room was cream-colored and covered with miniature garlands of small blue flowers. The flowers were faded and as indistinct as the real flowers in her garden were today in the rain. It was old wallpaper and, like the yellow rosebush, it had been here when she and Martin moved in, years ago.

All the windows in the house were closed tight against the rain, but the damp had crept in anyway. Mrs. Bagot turned from the window. Her feet and legs were cold—that was how people got rheumatism. On a day as bad as this, if the children were here, she would have lighted the fire hours ago, even if it was an extravagance. There was no use risking colds and coughs. She took the box of matches from the mantelpiece and knelt down on the hearthrug. It was between two and three weeks since they had needed a fire, and the coals were nearly hidden under a litter of tiny balls of paper, thrown in there, she knew, by Lily. She hated to burn them up. She took one ball and smoothed it out and, as she expected, it was a code. Lily was always hoping to discover a code that would be easy to write and impossible for anybody except herself to understand. Mrs. Bagot thought of taking the others out, just to look at them, but then she thought better of it. If she continued to think like this about the children she would bring bad luck on them. She struck the match impatiently and touched it here and there to the newspaper at the bottom of the grate. There were tears in her eyes. She wanted the children to enjoy themselves, but she wondered if they thought of her at all when they were away from her. They would be falling in love with their aunt and with their uncles. They would come back at the end of the month pining for the farm and the animals and all the freedom they had down there. Well, it couldn't be helped. Maybe it was all for the best.

She started to stand up, when a warm body touched her leg. It was Bennie, the white terrier, who had come out of his sleep on the rug beside the folding doors to hear a match being struck and a fire beginning. He looked up at her. He had small brown poverty-stricken eyes and limp ears, but the line from his black nose to his chin was fine and square, and she often told the children Bennie had very good blood in him. She put her arm around him and felt how close his bones were to the flat white coils of his fur. She wondered how old he was. You never could tell with a stray, and poor Bennie had been on his last legs when she found him on the street one morning on her way from Mass and took him home. She might have been able to walk past him, but some young boys were tormenting him, and she knew she would never be able to look herself in the face again if she abandoned him to their cruelty. He had been in the house five years now. Sometimes he seemed like a puppy and sometimes he was a very thoughtful, grown-up dog. He was very faithful. He had never once snapped at the children. He had never even snapped at the cats, although Rupert, the big orange one, was very greedy and often put his face into Bennies' food dish in the hope of finding a morsel there he might fancy for himself. "Good Bennie," Mrs. Bagot said, and pressed him closer to her side, and he stretched his neck up to her, and the storm of devotion in his eyes could never have found expression in speech. His silence burned with devotion, and so it would as long as he was alive.

She rubbed his shoulder and smiled at him and then she stood up. She moved easily, rising from her knees to stand with no effort, but when she was on her feet she felt dizzy. It was her own fault. She had not bothered to eat anything at breakfast time. She had had a cup of tea when she got up, and then, in the middle of the day, more tea, and that was all. She had felt angry with the children at breakfast time, because while she could feel angry she believed she did not miss them, and then, in the middle of the day, when her false anger, her pretense, had faded, she felt shame at the picture of herself going to trouble over food that the children would not be there to share.

Now then, she was going to have to stop thinking like that. She should know better by this time than to let herself fall into this train of thought. In the beginning, at the beginning of their marriage, Martin had warned her often enough against thinking, because thinking led to self-pity and there was enough of that in this world. What he had really told her was that she must stop forcing herself, stop *trying* to think, because her intelligence was not high and she must not put too much of a strain on it or she would make herself unhappy. "I don't want you to make yourself unhappy," he had said, and she remembered the nice tone his voice used to have when he spoke to her. Things had not been the same between them since Jimmy died. Jimmy would have been ten now—nearly three years older than Lily. Poor little mite, he had lived only three days, and she had not been herself for a long time afterward, and perhaps she had said things she shouldn't have said. She was sorry now for the things she shouldn't have said and that she couldn't clearly remember saying, but when she thought of that time, her mind turned to ether and she got all sleepy, and she knew it was unhealthy, not the right frame of mind for her to be in, and when the children were at home she was so busy with them that she had no time to let her thoughts go back. And she must always remember that Martin was very nice with Lily and Margaret, a very good father. He was very fond of them, and sometimes on Sunday afternoons he took them for a walk. He always asked Lily about her schoolwork, and took an interest in her. And he invented games for Margaret, to make her laugh. Lily took after him—she was very clever and always got good marks. Lily was a bit too sure of herself, perhaps, but she was a good child, and there would be a letter from her tomorrow, Mrs. Bagot was sure of that. Where the children were now, in the country, the postman went his rounds on a bicycle, and Lily would have been watching for him this afternoon.

It must be raining there, too, raining down on the trees and the fields and on the house where it stood at the end of the lane from the village. The lane was a mile long—a long ride for anyone on a bicycle—but the postman would have arrived, with the letter she had sent to them secretly the day before yesterday, when they were still here with her, and Lily would have been on the watch for him, to give him the letter for her mother. And the letter would come into Dublin on the night train, and it would be here in the morning. Well, Mrs. Bagot thought, with luck she would have it in the morning, but if it came in the morning post, she would have to give it to Martin— he would be sure to ask if there was a letter from Lily, so that he could take it along to the office to show his friends what a clever daughter he had. And then ten chances to one she would never see it again. It would stay there in the office and get mixed up in the papers on his desk and maybe be thrown out, unless someone took it. She would ask Martin to bring it back, and he would promise to bring it to her, but he would forget, and she might ask him the second time but not the third time—it was too much like nagging. And all this brought home to her how little she meant to anyone in the world except the children. And Bennie and the cats. Martin objected to the animals, and he had told her to get rid of them, but she refused to get rid of them. She had stood up to him there. Anyway, he hardly saw them. He woke up late, naturally enough, considering how late at night he had to work, and she brought him up his breakfast on a tray, and then he dressed himself and went off and came back in the early hours of the morning. He did not like her to wait up for him, and besides she couldn't and still get enough sleep to be able to give proper attention to the children. But she would always wait up for him if she thought that was what he wanted. But the times she had been up, when he got home at eleven o'clock, for example, instead of at one or two—at those times he had come in and hung his coat and hat in the hall and gone straight upstairs to his room without even saying good night to her. There were times when it seemed that he could not control his dislike of her, and yet she knew very well he did not dislike her. One night, not so very long ago, he had come into the front bedroom where she slept and waked her and asked her to heat up some milk for him, and when she brought him the milk he thanked her and told her he did not know what he would do without her. She had gone back to her own bed and lain there in an ecstasy of gratitude—a gratitude she did not understand and did not question. She knew positively that everything was going to be all right, and she was so sure of that—that everything was going to be all right—that she did not even wonder what she meant, or who or what it was she was thinking about. She only knew that her memory had lighted up and that all she remembered were times so happy that they must surely cast their radiance far into the future, over years so far ahead that she could not even dream of them.

Once, shortly after she and Martin were married, shortly after they moved to Dublin, she had wanted to get material for curtains for the back bedroom, which was still unfurnished then, because there were only the two of them in the house. Martin said he had heard of a good shop, and he volunteered to go with her, and he said, she remembered very well, that he would take her there and see that she had someone to wait on her but that then he would have to leave her, because he had an appointment. But when they got to the shop, he didn't leave her. He stayed and watched while the man behind the counter showed her what they had in the way of cretonne. The man behind the counter gave Mrs. Bagot a chair, but Martin refused to sit down. "I feel like a bull in a china shop," he said, "but at least I needn't be a sitting bull." They all laughed, and a woman standing nearby waiting for her parcel to be wrapped laughed and smiled at Mrs. Bagot, and the man behind the counter winked at Mrs. Bagot and said, "That is a witty man you have there, Mrs ..." And she had said "Mrs. Bagot," in such a high voice that Martin burst out laughing and said to the man behind the counter, "She's still surprised at her new name." And then Martin said, "We're only four months married," and he spoke so proudly that even she could see his pride, and she couldn't take her eyes off him—she looked at him, she gave him the same devoted, desperate look that Bennie always gave to her.

Yes, that day had been wonderful. After they left the shop the day did not end; they did not part. She was certain when they walked out onto the street that he would hurry away, and she was ready for that—to turn and go her own way home alone—but Martin said, looking up and down the crowded, busy street, "I could stand a cup of tea. What about you, Delia? After all this exertion you'd like a nice cup of tea, wouldn't you?" He was grinning at her, and then he said in a false, funny voice, "A nice cup of tea for the lady of the house?" Two or three times over the years, she had gone back to that tearoom, but the tables were always full, and so she had never gone in there again. The tea had been very good, and the cakes, and the girl had given them special attention, just as the man in the shop had done. And after tea they had gone for a walk, strolling around, looking in the shop windows, and when she reminded him of his appointment he said, "They can wait, I can see them anytime. But when will I get another chance to show you off like this?" It was strange that at the start of that long-ago day, when she got out of bed in the morning, she had not had a hint that she was seeing the beginning of a day that would never cease to unfold in her memory and that would always be waiting there, undimmed and undamaged, providing her with a place where her mind could rest and find courage.

Martin had given up sleeping in the big front bedroom, because she and the children got up early and disturbed him, moving about, and now he slept in the small room next to the bathroom, on the landing halfway up the stairs. Lately she had been hoping he would say something to her that would give them both a chance of a talk, but he had said nothing. She knew things were not as they should be between them, but while the children were at home she did not want to say anything for fear of a row that might frighten the children, and now that the children were away she found she was afraid to speak for fear of disturbing a silence that might, if broken, reveal any number of things that she did not want to see and that she was sure he did not want to see. Or perhaps he saw them and kept silent out of charity, or out of despair, or out of a hope that they would vanish if no one paid any attention to them.

But here she was now, doing herself no good—it was only storing up trouble to let herself get weak with hunger simply because she longed for a *real* reason to feel sorry for herself. She would make the toast and have tea with it. But before she did anything she would open the folding doors into the front sitting room and let some of the warmth of the fire steal in there. The room where she stood was less a dining room than a back sitting room, because she and the children spent their time there when they weren't in the kitchen. The leaves of the big table had been let down, and it stood flat against the wall, with a bowl of her roses on it from this morning. The floor was covered in linoleum, but the rug Bennie had been sleeping on before he crossed to lie in the warmth of the fire fitted very neatly under the folding doors, very much as though it had been specially made, and it gave the room a nice, well-furnished appearance. She opened the doors back carefully. The front room was dim. The curtains were still up on the windows in this room—long French windows that curved out into a bow—and the gray houses across the street were dark in the falling rain. Her own house, she supposed, looked dark to her neighbors over there. She saw that some of them had their lights on, although it was only five o'clock. There was an upright piano against the wall opposite the fireplace in this room. She had put a bowl of pink roses on the piano earlier in the day, and a small vase of them on the mantelpiece. She thought that what light there was in the room came from the roses and from the shining wood of the piano. Also, the fragrance of the roses was stronger in this room than in the back room where she had been standing for so long. Standing doing nothing, she thought. But instead of reproaching herself she went to the windows and looked out into the street, which was narrow and had two facing rows of houses, all identical with her own. She liked to watch people going up and down the street, and she sometimes came in here to attend to her collection of ferns so that she could watch what was going on outside without seeming curious.

The ferns, all of them tall and feathery and all in the same bright shade of green—bright moss green, grass green—were arranged on a table that stood inside the bow window. She had to leave a space between the two middle pots so that Minnie, the small black cat, could sleep there. Minnie's favorite spot was in the center of the table between the ferns, and if a suitable place was not left for her she would make one, squeezing herself in until the pots rattled dangerously. Minnie was there now, half asleep, and Mrs. Bagot stroked her and watched the street. The street was safe for the children to play in. It was a dead end, and there were no garages, and in any case very few of the people had cars. The milkman came early in the morning and the bread man at eleven, but otherwise Mrs. Bagot hardly ever had to open the front door, except for the children when they came home from school at half past three. At noon every day she walked to the school with the children's lunch.

The school was not far away—a short walk along the main road and then a longer walk down a side street that was wider and busier than this one, with much bigger houses, except at the end, where the houses were suddenly very small and close together. The school was across from the small houses, behind a high cement wall with a narrow iron gate in its center. The gate opened into a cement yard, where the children played at lunchtime, and the school building, gray and high, with a few large, oblong, institutional windows, fitted and matched the yard exactly, as though a child had drawn and colored it. The yard was completely closed in by high cement walls, and to the right, looking from the gate, there was a very long, low wooden bench where the smallest children sometimes sat in a row and did their lessons. There were children in the school who were no more than three years old, and some of them, Mrs. Bagot suspected, were only two. But they were able to walk—that was all the school required—and Mrs. Bagot would not have admitted to anyone that one of her reasons for going to the trouble of bringing Lily and Margaret their lunch every day was so that she could see the little boys and girls who were just able to walk. The little ones were let out to play before the rest of the school, and by the time she got to the gate they were generally running around, stumbling like moths from one side of the yard to the other and beating at the air with their hands, and looking up at their teacher as though they imagined she produced the light by which they played. There was no one to question Mrs. Bagot's right to stand and watch the children. If anyone questioned her she would simply say she had to bring Lily and Margaret their lunch. Well, there would be no bringing lunch for a while. It would be more than five weeks before they had to go back to school.

Mrs. Bagot turned from the street and from Minnie and from the ferns, and was surprised to see how like a mirror the big naked window in the back room was, but like a mirror that you could see through, a mirror that went both ways and showed both sides. It was like a painting. She saw the wet, reluctant daylight air out there in the garden, and the rain was falling so strong and straight that she was sure she could make out every separate driving line of it. Beyond and through the rain, as in a dream, there were the indistinct colors of the garden, and then, coming back through the glass to herself, she could see herself, with the folded-back door to her right, and behind her the wavering green heads of her ferns, and behind the ferns the starched white net curtains making a ghostly and final wall. She knew that what she saw was beautiful, and at the same moment she knew that she did not want to look anymore at the window or the garden or the ferns or anything. She was tired. She hurried out of the room and down to the kitchen, where she filled the kettle and put it on to boil for her tea. While the kettle was boiling she would wash her face and hands and straighten her hair. The cold water on her face would wake her up—she felt that she had been sleeping for hours, and not sleeping happily. She hurried upstairs. The narrow stairs from the hall had a wine-red runner that was held in place at each step by thin brass rods that she pulled out and polished every Monday. The rods shone more steadily in this evening's dimness than they ever shone on a sunny day, and the wooden banister glowed with the same warm and reverberating depth, as though the dying light called up sources of strength that went unnoticed in the self-sufficient daytime. The house was full of secret light that she never noticed when the children were at home.

After washing her hands, she hurried up the five top steps to the upper landing, where there were two doors opening into the front bedroom and into the smaller back room where the children slept. Both doors were closed, and instead of going into her own room, where her brush and comb were, she turned into the children's room and went across and looked into the small framed mirror that stood on their chest of drawers. She began to smooth her hair with her hands, but her reflection was so lost and pale that it frightened her, and she put on the light to reassure herself. She bent forward to the mirror again and carefully pushed a loose strand into the neat bun at the back of her head, but as she moved, something moved with her, something much larger and even more silent than she was. Her shadow was on the wall to the side of the mirror and it was following her, and now it was bending with her, bending toward her, and she stared at it. The light in her own bedroom gave her no shadow that she had ever noticed. She paused and the shadow paused also, waiting for her as she waited for it. She looked closer and at that moment, as it bent its head, she knew what she was looking at. That was her mother's shadow there on the wall. There was no mistake about it; that was her mother.

Mrs. Bagot could not understand it. She and her mother had not looked alike. But there it was, her mother's shadow as she had often seen it—the thin line of the cheek, the indentation at the eye, the high curve of the forehead, and, above all, the little straying hairs that always escaped the brush to wave independently at the sides of her mother's forehead and at the back of her neck. The little stray hairs were never more than the length of a straight pin, and there were only a few of them. Mrs. Bagot thought she recognized every one of them, there in the shadow. She thought that if she put out her hand she would surely feel that hair again. She put out the light and then put it on again at once. There again was the neat, bent head, with the thin hairs making a frail pattern on the wall, a frail pattern that was more real at this moment than the pattern on the wallpaper, as the penciled rain in a Chinese watercolor is more real than the strong and enduring landscape that lies beyond. It is my mother, Mrs. Bagot thought; there she is, how patient she is.

She sighed once and smiled at herself without looking at herself, and then she put out the light and went down to the kitchen, where she found the kettle boiling furiously.

The tea was soon made and so was the toast. She took down Martin's breakfast tray and set it carefully for herself, even putting a clean white cloth on it, but when everything was arranged, instead of carrying the tray up to the fireside, she pulled a chair up to the kitchen table and sat down and poured herself a cup of tea. She was too hungry and too thirsty. She could stand no further delay; she must have something to eat at once. She thought about the shadow that had been waiting for her up there in the children's room all these years and that had remained hidden from her until tonight. She had never seen it in any other room in the house and she did not think it was to be seen in any other room of the house.

She looked around her, but the shadow was not in the kitchen. Bennie was sitting on the tiled floor at her feet, and she broke off a piece of toast and gave it to him. Rupert and Minnie had suddenly appeared and were sitting thoughtfully beside their milk saucer near the door that led out into the garden. She got up and poured milk for the cats, and then she went back to the table and poured herself another cup of tea. She decided to make more toast, and to eat some of the chicken that was left over from the special dinner she had made for the children yesterday. She felt all different—not sad, not tired anymore. She felt very hopeful all of a sudden. It was wonderful how seeing that shadow had raised her spirits. It was wonderful knowing that shadow was upstairs and that it would never go away. It was almost like having somebody in the house.

Rose-Coloured Teacups

A. S. Byatt

There were three women in the room, two sitting in low, oval-backed armchairs, and one on the end of a bed, her pale head lit by a summer window, her face slightly shadowed. They were young women, full of energy; this could be seen in the quick, alert turns of the heads, the movements of hand to mouth, carrying a cigarette in a long holder, a rose-coloured teacup. They wore knee-length shifts, one olive, one russet (sometimes it was a kind of dull crimson), one, belonging to the pale head, a clotted cream or blanket-wool colour. They all had smooth but not shining pale stockings and barred, buttoned shoes, with pointed toes and very small heels. One dark woman, in a chair, had long hair, knotted in the nape of her neck. The other two were shingled. The pale-headed woman, when she turned her head to look out of the window, could be seen to have the most beautiful slanting ledge of shorn silver and gold from the turn of her skull to the fine neck. She had a fine-edged upper lip, still and calm; a composed look, but expectant. The third woman was harder to see; the haircut was decisive and mannish; Veronica had to resist seeing it as she had always known it, pepper and salt.

She could see the chairs very clearly, one with a pale green linen cover, fitted, and one with a creased chintz, covered with large, floppy roses. She could see the little fire, with its dusty coal scuttle and brass fire-irons. Sometimes she saw it burning brightly, but mostly it was dark, because it was summer outside, and through the window, between the rosy chintz curtains, there was the unchanging college garden with its rosebeds and packed herbaceous border, its sunken pool and smell of mown grass. There were leaves coiling into the picture round the outside of the window-frame—a climbing rose, a creeper, what was it? She could see a desk, not very clearly. It was no good straining to see; it was necessary to wait quietly. There was a dark corner containing a piece of furniture she had never managed to see at all—a wardrobe? She could always see the low table, set for tea. There was a little kettle, on a trivet, and a capacious sprigged teapot, a walnut cake, on a plate, slices of malt loaf, six pink lustre teacups, rosily iridescent, with petal-shaped saucers. The lustre glaze streaked the strong pink with cobwebs of blue-grey and white-gold. And little butter knives with blunt ends and ivory handles there would be, there were, and a little cut glass dish of butter. And one of jam, yes, with a special flat jam spoon. The women talked to each other. They were waiting for someone. She could not hear their conversation or their occasional laughter. She could see the tablecloth, white linen with a drawn threadwork border, and thick embroidered flowers spilling in swags round its edges, done in that embroidery silk that is dyed in deepening and paler shades of the same colour. She mostly saw the flowers as roses, though many of them, looked at more closely, were hybrid or imaginary creations. She was overdoing the pink.

Her daughter Jane called from upstairs, peremptory and wailing. Jane was unusually at home because of some unexpected hiatus in her very busy social life, which flowed and overflowed from house to house, from friend's kitchen to friend's kitchen, loud with rock, pungent with illegal smoke, vigorous-voiced. Jane had decided to sew something. The sewing-machine was in the spare bedroom. She appeared to be slicing up a pillowcase and reconstructing it into the curiously formed bandeaux and rag-ribbons that went with certain versions of her hair. The sewing-machine had given up, Jane said, it was a stupid thing. She sat at the sewing-table and gave the machine a decisive slap, looking up with her extravagant face surrounded by a rayed sooty star of erect and lacquered hair, a jagged work of art. She had her father's big black eyes, outlined in kohl, and Veronica's father's wide and shapely mouth, painted a glossy magenta. She was big and compact, round and slender, very much alive, a woman and a cross child. It wouldn't *pick up*, the needle, Jane said, rattling the wheel round and round, clattering antique pistons and hinges. It was the tension. The tension had gone to pot. She pulled furiously at the pieces of rag and thread whirred out of the underparts of the machine where the shuttle bustled and nattered. The top thread was snapped. Veronica's mother had had the machine as a wedding present in 1930; it had been second-hand then. Veronica had had it since 1960, when Jane's elder sister had been born. She had made baby clothes on it and nightdresses. Only simple things. She was no seamstress. Her mother had been only moderately efficient with the thing, though she had used it to make do in the war, turning collars, cutting down trousers, making coats into skirts, and curtains into dungarees. Her mother's mother had been a dressmaker in the 1890s. And had also done hand-embroidery, cushions and handtowels, handkerchiefs and 'runners' for dresser-tops.

Jane tugged at her multiple earrings, coils of gold wire and little glass beads. I had a go at the tension, she said. I can't get it to go back. Jane was forthright and attacking with many things Veronica had her generation's classic inadequacy about: machines, group living, authority. Jane inhabited a mechanical world. She walked the pavements with a pendant black box, she lived amongst a festoon of electricity, hi-fi, hairdryer, tape-deck, curling-tongs, crimper. She had undone the tension-gauge on the elderly Swan Vickers and spattered various metal discs over the sewing-table. She had become irritated with the irregular coil of fine wire, with its needle-eye hook at the end, on which the thread bobs jerkily and peacefully when the machine is in running order. She had tugged and jerked at it, teasing it out of its coil so that it now protruded, a wavering, threatening, disconnected spike, pointing out nowhere.

Veronica felt rage. She said, "But that is a coiled *spring*, Jane—" and heard in her mind's ear a preliminary ghost of her own voice about to embark on a howling plaint, how *could* you, have you no feelings, my mother kept that machine all her life, I always looked after it, it was cared for …

And abruptly remembered her own mother's voice in the 1950s, unrestrained, wailing, interminable, how *could* you, how *could* you, and saw briefly the pair of them, her mother with her miserable disappointed face, the mouth set in a down-droop, and her own undergraduate self, sugar-petticoated, smooth-skinned, eye-lined and passionate, staring at the shards of pink lustre teacups in a road-delivered teachest. The teacups had been given by her mother's old college friend, to take back a new generation to the college. She had not liked the teacups. She did not like pink, and the floral shape of the saucers was most unfashionable. She and her friends drank Nescafe from stone mugs or plain cylinders in primary colours. She had left folded in her drawer the tablecloth embroidered for her by her grandmother, whose style of embroidery was now exemplified by the cloth, so stiff and clean and brilliant, in the visionary teaparty she had taken to imagining since her mother died. It was a curious form of mourning, but compulsive, and partly comforting. It seemed to be all she was capable of. The force of her mother's rage against the house and housewifery that trapped her and, by extension, against her clever daughters, who had all partly evaded that trap, precluded wholehearted mourning. The silence of her absence was like coming in out of a storm. Or like the silence of that still little room, in its bright expectancy, one or any afternoon in the late 1920s.

She could not reproduce that fury against Jane. She repeated, "It's a spring, you can't uncoil it" and Jane said half-heartedly that she didn't see why not, and they sat down together to try to make sense of the scattered parts of the tension-regulator.

Veronica remembered packing the pink cups. Something had been terribly wrong. She remembered moving around her college room in a daze of defeat and anguish barely summoning up the strength to heap the despised crockery, all anyhow, into the crate, thinking that there should have been newspaper to wrap things in and that she didn't have any. And that the effort of finding any was beyond her. But although she could remember the fine frenzy in which the fate of the teacups had seemed immaterial, the cause was gone. Had she lost a lover? Missed a part in a university play? Said something and regretted it? Feared pregnancy? Or had it been merely vaguer fears of meaninglessness and inertia which had assailed her then, when she was lively, and had been replaced now by the stiffer and more precise fears of death and never getting things done? The girl in her memory of that passively miserable day's packing seemed discontinuous with herself—looked in on, as much as the imaginary teaparty. She could remember vividly taking a furtive look through a door in the part of the college where her mother's room had been, and seeing two low chairs and a bed under a window. The chairs in her constructed vision were draped anachronistically in the loose covers they had worn in her brief, half-reluctant glimpse of them. Her mother had wanted her to be at the college and had felt excluded, then, by her daughter's presence there, from her own memories of the place. The past had been made into the past, discontinuous from the present. It had been a fantasy that Veronica would sit in the same chairs, in the same sunlight and drink from the same cups. No one steps into the same river twice. Jane's elder sister, Veronica's elder daughter, had also gone to the college, and Veronica, forewarned, had watched her assert her place in it, her here and now.

The telephone rang. Jane said that would be Barnaby and her cross lassitude fell away. At the door on the way out, she turned and said to Veronica, "I'm sorry about the machine. I'm sure it'll mend. And anyway it's geriatric." She could be heard singing on the stairs, on the way to the telephone, to take up her life again. She sang beautifully in a large clear voice, inherited from her father, who could sing, and not from Veronica and her mother who scraped tunelessly. She was singing in the Brahms Requiem in the school choir. She rolled out joyfully, "Lord make me to know mine end, and the measure of my days, what it is; that I may know, that I may know how frail I am."

The three women sat in the little room, imagined not remembered. Veronica detected in her mother's cream-coloured dress just a touch of awkwardness, her grandmother's ineptness at a trade for which she was not wholly suited, a shoulder out of true, a cuff awry, as so many buttons and cuffs and waistbands had been during the making-do in the time of austerity. This awkwardness in her mother was lovable and vulnerable. The other shingled woman raised the teapot and poured amber tea into rosy teacups. Two of these cups and one saucer, what was salvaged, stood now on Veronica's dresser, useless and, Veronica thought, exquisitely pretty. Her mother raised her pale head expectantly, lifting that fine lip, fixing her whole attention on the door, through which they came—Veronica could see so much—the young men in blazers and wide flannels, college scarves and smoothed hair, smiling decorously. Veronica saw him smile with the wide and shapely smile that had just reappeared, deprecating and casual, on Jane's different, darker face. She saw the little, blonde, pretty face in the window lit with pure pleasure, pure hope, almost content. She could never see any further: from there, it always began again, chairs, tablecloth, sunny window, rosy teacups, a safe place.

Love Is Not a Pie

Amy Bloom

In the middle of the eulogy at my mother's boring and heartbreaking funeral, I began to think about calling off the wedding. August 21 did not seem like a good date, John Wescott did not seem like a good person to marry, and I couldn't see myself in the long white silk gown Mrs. Wescott had offered me. We had gotten engaged at Christmas, while my mother was starting to die; she died in May, earlier than we had expected. When the minister said, "She was a rare spirit, full of the kind of bravery and joy which inspires others," I stared at the pale blue ceiling and thought, "My mother would not have wanted me to spend my life with this man." He had asked me if I wanted him to come to the funeral from Boston, and I said no. And so he didn't, respecting my autonomy and so forth. I think he should have known that I was just being considerate.

After the funeral, we took the little box of ashes back to the house and entertained everybody who came by to pay their respects. Lots of my father's law school colleagues, a few of his former students, my uncle Steve and his new wife, my cousins (whom my sister Lizzie and I always referred to as Thing One and Thing Two), friends from the old neighborhood, before my mother's sculpture started selling, her art world friends, her sisters, some of my friends from high school, some people I used to baby-sit for, my best friend from college, some friends of Lizzie's, a lot of people I didn't recognize. I'd been living away from home for a long time, first at college, now at law school.

My sister, my father, and I worked the room. And everyone who came in my father embraced. It didn't matter whether they started to pat him on the back or shake his hand, he pulled them to him and hugged them so hard I saw people's feet lift right off the floor. Lizzie and I took the more passive route, letting people do whatever they wanted to us, patting, stroking, embracing, cupping our faces in their hands.

My father was in the middle of squeezing Mrs. Ellis, our cleaning lady, when he saw Mr. DeCuervo come in, still carrying his suitcase. He about dropped Mrs. Ellis and went charging over to Mr. DeCuervo, wrapped his arms around him, and the two of them moaned and rocked together in a passionate, musicless waltz. My sister and I sat down on the couch, pressed against each other, watching our father cry all over his friend, our mother's lover.

When I was eleven and Lizzie was eight, her last naked summer, Mr. DeCuervo and his daughter, Gisela, who was just about to turn eight, spent part of the summer with us at the cabin in Maine. The cabin was from the Spencer side, my father's side of the family, and he and my uncle Steve were co-owners. We went there every July (colder water, better weather), and they came in August. My father felt about his brother the way we felt about our cousins, so we would only overlap for lunch on the last day of our stay.

That July, the DeCuervos came, but without Mrs. DeCuervo, who had to go visit a sick someone in Argentina, where they were from. That was okay with us. Mrs. DeCuervo was a professional mother, a type that made my sister and me very uncomfortable. She told us to wash the berries before we ate them, to rest after lunch, to put on more sun tan lotion, to make our beds. She was a nice lady, she was just always in our way. My mother had a few very basic summer rules:

don't eat food with mold or insects on it; don't swim alone; don't even think about waking your mother before 8:00 A.M., unless you are fatally injured or ill. That was about it, but Mrs. DeCuervo was always amending and adding to the list, one apologetic eye on our mother, who was pleasant and friendly as usual and did things the way she always did. She made it pretty clear that if we were cowed by the likes of Mrs. DeCuervo, we were on our own. They got divorced when Gisela was a sophomore at Mount Holyoke.

We liked pretty, docile Gisela, and bullied her a little bit, and liked her even more because she didn't squeal on us, on me in particular. We liked her father, too. We saw the two of them, sometimes the three of them, at occasional picnics and lesser holidays. He always complimented us, never made stupid jokes at our expense, and brought us unusual, perfect little presents. Silver barrettes for me the summer I was letting my hair grow out from my pixie cut; a leather bookmark for Lizzie, who learned to read when she was three. My mother would stand behind us as we unwrapped the gifts, smiling and shaking her head at his extravagance.

When they drove up, we were all sitting on the porch. Mr. DeCuervo got out first, his curly brown hair making him look like a giant dandelion, with his yellow t-shirt and brown jeans. Gisela looked just like him, her long, curly brown hair caught up in a bun, wisps flying around her tanned little face. As they walked toward us, she took his hand and I felt a rush of warmth for her, for showing how much she loved her daddy, like I loved mine, and for showing that she was a little afraid of us, of me, probably. People weren't often frightened of Lizzie; she never left her books long enough to bother anyone.

My parents came down from the porch; my big father, in his faded blue trunks, drooping below his belly, his freckled back pink and moist in the sun, as it was every summer. The sun caught the red hair on his head and shoulders and chest, and he shone. The Spencers were half-Viking, he said. My mother was wearing her summer outfit, a black two-piece bathing suit. I don't remember her ever wearing a different suit. At night, she'd add one of my father's shirts and wrap it around her like a kimono. Some years, she looked great in her suit, waist nipped in, skin smooth and tan; other years, her skin looked burnt and crumpled, and the suit was too big in some places and too small in others. Those years, she smoked too much and went out on the porch to cough. But that summer the suit fit beautifully, and when she jumped off the porch into my father's arms, he whirled her around and let her black hair whip his face while he smiled and smiled.

They both hugged Mr. DeCuervo and Gisela; my mother took her flowered suitcase and my father took his duffel bag and they led them into the cabin.

The cabin was our palace; Lizzie and I would say very grandly, "We're going to the cabin for the summer, come visit us there, if it's okay with your parents." And we loved it and loved to act as though it was nothing special, when we knew, really, that it was magnificent. The pines and birches came right down to the lake, with just a thin lacing of mossy rocks before you got to the smooth cold water, and little gray fish swam around the splintery dock and through our legs, or out of reach of our oars when we took out the old blue rowboat.

The cabin itself was three bedrooms and a tiny kitchen and a living room that took up half the house. The two small bedrooms had big beds with pastel chenille spreads; yellow with red roses in my parents' room, white with blue pansies in the other. The kids' room was much bigger, like a dormitory, with three sets of bunk beds, each with its own mismatched sheets and pillowcases. The pillows were always a little damp and smelled like salt and pine, and mine smelled of Ma Griffe as well, because I used to sleep with my mother's scarf tucked under it. The shower was outside, with a thin green plastic curtain around it, but there was a regular bathroom inside, next to my parents' room.

Mr. DeCuervo and Gisela fit into our routine as though they'd been coming to the cabin for years, instead of just last summer. We had the kind of summer cabin routine that stays with you forever as a model of leisure, of life being enjoyed. We'd get up early, listening to the birds screaming and trilling, and make ourselves some breakfast; cereal or toast if the parents were up, cake or cold spaghetti or marshmallows if they were still asleep. My mother got up first, usually. She'd make a cup of coffee and brush and braid our hair and set us loose. If we were going exploring, she'd put three sandwiches and three pieces of fruit in a bag, with an army blanket. Otherwise, she'd just wave to us as we headed down to the lake.

We'd come back at lunchtime and eat whatever was around and then go out to the lake or the forest, or down the road to see if the townie kids were in a mood to play with us. I don't know what the grown-ups did all day; sometimes they'd come out to swim for a while, and sometimes we'd find my mother in the shed she used for a studio. But when we came back at five or six, they all seemed happy and relaxed, drinking gin and tonics on the porch, watching us run toward the house. It was the most beautiful time.

At night, after dinner, the fathers would wash up and my mother would sit on the porch, smoking a cigarette, listening to Aretha Franklin or Billie Holiday or Sam Cooke, and after a little while she'd stub out her cigarette and the four of us would dance. We'd twist and lindy and jitterbug and stomp, all of us copying my mother. And pretty soon the daddies would drift in with their dish towels and their beers, and they'd lean in the doorway and watch. My mother would turn first to my father, always to him, first.

"What about it, Danny? Care to dance?" And she'd put her hand on his shoulder and he'd smile, tossing his dish towel to Mr. DeCuervo, resting his beer on the floor. My father would lumber along gamely, shuffling his feet and smiling. Sometimes he'd wave his arms around and pretend to be a fish or a bear while my mother swung her body easily and dreamily, sliding through the music. They'd always lindy together to Fats Domino. That was my father's favorite, and then he'd sit down, puffing a little.

My mother would stand there, snapping her fingers, shifting back and forth.

"Gaucho, you dance with her, before I have a coronary," said my father.

Mr. DeCuervo's real name was Bolivar, which I didn't know until Lizzie told me after the funeral. We always called him Mr. DeCuervo because we felt embarrassed to call him by a nickname.

So Mr. DeCuervo would shrug gracefully and toss the two dish towels back to my father. And then he'd bop toward my mother, his face still turned toward my father.

"We'll go running tomorrow, Dan, get you back into shape so you can dance all night."

"What do you mean, 'back'? I've been exactly this same svelte shape for twenty years. Why fix it if it ain't broke?"

And they all laughed, and Mr. DeCuervo and my mother rolled their eyes at each other, and my mother walked over and kissed my father where the sweat was beading up at his temples. Then she took Mr. DeCuervo's hand and they walked to the center of the living room.

When she and my father danced, my sister and I giggled and interfered and treated it like a family badminton game in which they were the core players but we were welcome participants. When she danced with Mr. DeCuervo, we'd sit on the porch swing or lean on the windowsill and watch, not even looking at each other.

They only danced the fast dances, and they danced as though they'd been waiting all their lives for each song. My mother's movements got deeper and smoother, and Mr. DeCuervo suddenly came alive, as though a spotlight had hit him. My father danced the way he was, warm, noisy, teasing, a little overpowering; but Mr. DeCuervo, who was usually quiet and thoughtful and serious, became a different man when he danced with my mother. His dancing was light and happy and soulful, edging up on my mother, turning her, matching her every step. They would smile at all of us, in turn, and then face each other, too transported to smile.

"Dance with Daddy some more," my sister said, speaking for all three of us. They had left us too far behind.

My mother blew Lizzie a kiss. "Okay, sweetheart."

She turned to both men, laughing, and said, "That message was certainly loud and clear. Let's take a little break, Gauch, and get these monkeys to bed. It's getting late, girls."

And the three of them shepherded the three of us through the bedtime rituals, moving us in and out of the kitchen for milk, the bathroom for teeth, toilet, and calamine lotion, and finally to our big bedroom. We slept in our underwear and t-shirts, which impressed Gisela.

"No pajamas?" she had said the first night.

"Not necessary," I said smugly.

We would lie there after they kissed us, listening to our parents talk and crack peanuts and snap cards; they played gin and poker while they listened to Dinah Washington and Odetta.

One night, I woke up around midnight and crossed the living room to get some water in the kitchen and see if there was any strawberry shortcake left. I saw my mother and Mr. DeCuervo hugging, and I remember being surprised, and puzzled. I had seen movies; if you hugged someone like you'd never let them go, surely you were supposed to be kissing, too. It wasn't a Mommy-Daddy hug, partly because their hugs were defined by the fact that my father was eight inches taller and a hundred pounds heavier than my mother. These two looked all wrong to me; embraces were a big pink-and-orange man enveloping a small, lean black-and-white woman who gazed up at him. My mother and Mr. DeCuervo looked like sister and brother, standing cheek-to-cheek, with their broad shoulders and long, tanned, bare legs. My mother's hands were under Mr. DeCuervo's white t-shirt.

She must have felt my eyes on her, because she opened hers slowly.

"Oh, honey, you startled us. Mr. DeCuervo and I were just saying good night. Do you want me to tuck you in after you go to the bathroom?" Not quite a bribe, certainly a reminder that I was more important to her than he was. They had moved apart so quickly and smoothly I couldn't even remember how they had looked together. I nodded to my mother; what I had seen was already being transformed into a standard good-night embrace, the kind my mother gave to all of her close friends.

When I came back from the bathroom, Mr. DeCuervo had disappeared and my mother was waiting, looking out at the moon. She walked me to the bedroom and kissed me, first on my forehead, then on my lips.

"Sleep well, pumpkin pie. See you in the morning."

"Will you make blueberry pancakes tomorrow?" It seemed like a good time to ask.

"We'll see. Go to sleep."

"Please, Mommy."

"Okay, we'll have a blueberry morning. Go to sleep now. Good night, nurse." And she watched me for a moment from the doorway, and then she was gone.

My father got up at five to go fishing with some men at the other side of the lake. Every Saturday in July he'd go off with a big red bandanna tied over his bald spot, his Mets t-shirt, and his tackle box, and he'd fish until around three. Mr. DeCuervo said that he'd clean them, cook them, and eat them but he wouldn't spend a day with a bunch of guys in baseball caps and white socks to catch them.

I woke up smelling coffee and butter. Gisela and Lizzie were already out of bed, and I was aggrieved; I was the one who had asked for the pancakes, and they were probably all eaten by now.

Mr. DeCuervo and Lizzie were sitting at the table, finishing their pancakes. My mother and Gisela were sitting on the blue couch in the living room while my mother brushed Gisela's hair. She was brushing it more gently than she brushed mine, not slapping her on the shoulder to make her sit still. Gisela didn't wiggle, and she didn't scream when my mother hit a knot.

I was getting ready to be mad when my mother winked at me over Gisela's head and said, "There's a stack of pancakes for you on top of the stove, bunny. Gauch, would you please lift them for Ellen? The plate's probably hot."

Mr. DeCuervo handed me my pancakes, which were huge brown wheels studded with smashed purpley berries; he put my fork and knife on top of a folded paper towel and patted my cheek. His hand smelled like coffee and cinnamon. He knew what I liked and pushed the butter and the honey and the syrup toward me.

"Juice?" he said.

I nodded, trying to watch him when he wasn't looking; he didn't seem like the man I thought I saw in the moonlight, giving my mother a funny hug.

"Great pancakes, Lila," he said.

"Great, Mom." I didn't want to be outclassed by the DeCuervos' habitual good manners. Gisela remembered her "please" and "thank you" for every little thing.

My mother smiled and put a barrette in Gisela's hair. It was starting to get warm, so I swallowed my pancakes and kicked Lizzie to get her attention.

"Let's go," I said.

"Wash your face, then go," my mother said.

I stuck my face under the kitchen tap, and my mother and Mr. DeCuervo laughed. Triumphantly, I led the two little girls out of the house, snatching our towels off the line as we ran down to the water, suddenly filled with longing for the lake.

"Last one in's a fart," I screamed, cannonballing off the end of the dock. I hit the cold blue water, shattering its surface. Lizzie and Gisela jumped in beside me, and we played water games until my father drove up in the pickup with a bucket of fish. He waved to us and told us we'd be eating fish for the next two days, and we groaned and held our noses as he went into the cabin, laughing.

There was a string of sunny days like that one: swimming, fishing with Daddy off the dock, eating peanut butter and jelly sandwiches in the rowboat, drinking Orange Crush on the porch swing.

And then it rained for a week. We woke up the first rainy morning, listening to it tap and dance on the roof. My mother stuck her head into our bedroom.

"It's monsoon weather, honeys. How about cocoa and cinnamon toast?"

We pulled on our overalls and sweaters and went into the kitchen, where my mother had already laid our mugs and plates. She was engaged in her rainy day ritual: making Sangria. First she poured the orange juice out of the big white plastic pitcher into three empty peanut butter jars. Then she started chopping up all the oranges, lemons, and limes we had in the house. She let me pour the brandy over the fruit, Gisela threw in the sugar, and Lizzie came up for air long enough to pour the big bottle of red wine over everything. I cannot imagine drinking anything else on rainy days.

My mother went out onto the porch for her morning cigarette, and when my father came down he joined her while we played Go Fish; I could see them snuggling on the wicker settee. A few minutes later Mr. DeCuervo came down, looked out to the porch, and picked up an old magazine and started reading.

We decided to go play Monopoly in our room since the grown-ups didn't want to entertain us. After two hours, in which I rotted in jail and Lizzie forgot to charge rent, little Gisela beat us and the three of us went back to the kitchen for a snack. Rainy days were basically a series of snacks, more and less elaborate, punctuated by board games, card games, and whining. We drank soda and juice all day, ate cheese, bananas, cookies, bologna, graham crackers, Jiffy popcorn, hard-boiled eggs. The grown-ups ate cheese and crackers and drank sangria.

The daddies were reading in the two big armchairs, my mother had gone off to her room to sketch, and we were getting bored. When my mother came downstairs for a cigarette, I was writing my name in the honey that had spilled on the kitchen table, and Gisela and Lizzie were pulling the stuffing out of the hole in the bottom of the blue couch.

"Jesus Christ, Ellen, get your hands out of the goddamn honey. Liz, Gisela, that's absolutely unacceptable, you know that. Leave the poor couch alone. If you're so damn stir-crazy, go outside and dance in the rain."

The two men looked up, slowly focusing, as if from a great distance.

"Lila, really…," said my father.

"Lila, it's pouring. We'll keep an eye on them now," said Mr. DeCuervo.

"Right. Like you were." My mother was grinning.

"Can we, Mommy, can we go in the rain? Can we take off our clothes and go in the rain?"

"Sure, go naked, there's no point in getting your clothes wet and no point in suits. There's not likely to be a big crowd in the yard."

We raced to the porch before my mother could get rational, stripped and ran whooping into the rain, leaping off the porch onto the muddy lawn, shouting and feeling superior to every child in Maine who had to stay indoors.

We played Goddesses-in-the-Rain, which consisted of caressing our bodies and screaming the names of everyone we knew, and we played ring-around-the-rosy and tag and red light/green light and catch, all deliriously slippery and surreal in the sheets of gray rain. Our parents watched us from the porch.

When we finally came in, thrilled with ourselves and the extent to which we were completely, profoundly wet, in every pore, they bundled us up and told us to dry our hair and get ready for dinner.

My mother brushed our hair, and then she made spaghetti sauce while my father made a salad and Mr. DeCuervo made a strawberry tart, piling the berries into a huge, red, shiny pyramid in the center of the pastry. We were in heaven. The grownups were laughing a lot, sipping their rosy drinks, tossing vegetables back and forth.

After dinner, my mother took us into the living room to dance, and then the power went off.

"Shit," said my father in the kitchen.

"Double shit," said Mr. DeCuervo, and we heard them stumbling around in the dark, laughing and cursing, until they came in with two flashlights.

"The cavalry is here, ladies," said Daddy, bowing to us all, twirling his flashlight.

"American and Argentine divisions, señora y señoritas."

I had never heard Mr. DeCuervo speak Spanish before, not even that little bit.

"Well then, I know I'm safe—from the bad guys, anyway. On the other hand ..." My mother laughed, and the daddies put their arms around each other and they laughed too.

"On the other hand, what? What, Mommy?" I tugged at her the way I did when I was afraid of losing her in a big department store.

"Nothing, honey. Mommy was just being silly. Let's get ready for bed, munchkins. Then you can all talk for a while. We're shut down for the night, I'm sure."

The daddies accompanied us to the bathroom and whispered that we could skip everything except peeing, since there was no electricity.

The two of them kissed us good night, my father's mustache tickling, Mr. DeCuervo's sliding over my cheek. My mother came into the room a moment later, and her face was as smooth and warm as a velvet cushion. We didn't stay awake for long. The rain dance and the eating and the storm had worn us out.

It was still dark when I woke up, but the rain had stopped and the power had returned and the light was burning in our hallway. It made me feel very grown-up and responsible, getting out of bed and going around the house, turning out the lights that no one else knew were on; I was conserving electricity.

I went into the bathroom and was squeezed by stomach cramps, probably from all the burnt popcorn kernels I had eaten. I sat on the toilet for a long time, watching a brown spider crawl along the wall; I'd knock him down and then watch him climb back up again, toward the towels. My cramps were better but not gone, so I decided to wake my mother. My father would have been more sympathetic, but he was the heavier sleeper, and by the time he understood what I was telling him, my mother would have her bathrobe on and be massaging my stomach kindly, though without the excited concern I felt was my due as a victim of illness.

I walked down to my parents' room, turning the hall light back on. I pushed open the creaky door and saw my mother spooned up against my father's back, as she always was, and Mr. DeCuervo spooned up against her, his arm over the covers, his other hand resting on the top of her head.

I stood and looked and then backed out of the bedroom. They hadn't moved, the three of them breathing deeply, in unison. What was that, I thought, what did I see? I wanted to go back and take another look, to see it again, to make it disappear, to watch them carefully, until I understood.

My cramps were gone. I went back to my own bed, staring at Lizzie and Gisela, who looked in their sleep like little girl-versions of the two men I had just seen. Just sleeping, I thought, the grown-ups were just sleeping. Maybe Mr. DeCuervo's bed had collapsed, like ours did two summers ago. Or maybe it got wet in the storm. I thought I would never be able to fall asleep, but the next thing I remember is waking up to more rain and Lizzie and Gisela begging my mother to take us to the movies in town. We went to see *The Sound of Music*, which had been playing at the Bijou for about ten years.

I don't remember much else about the summer; all of the images run together. We went on swimming and fishing and taking the rowboat out for little adventures, and when the DeCuervos left I hugged Gisela but wasn't going to hug him, until he whispered in my ear, "Next year we'll bring up a motorboat and I'll teach you to water ski," and then I hugged him very hard and my mother put her hand on my head lightly, giving benediction.

The next summer, I went off to camp in July and wasn't there when the DeCuervos came. Lizzie said they had a good time without me. Then they couldn't come for a couple of summers in a row, and by the time they came again, Gisela and Lizzie were at camp with me in New Hampshire; the four grown-ups spent about a week together, and later I heard my father say that another vacation with Elvira DeCuervo would kill him, or he'd kill her. My mother said she wasn't so bad.

We saw them a little less after that. They came, Gisela and Mr. DeCuervo, to my high school graduation, to my mother's opening in Boston, my father's fiftieth birthday party, and then Lizzie's graduation. When my mother went down to New York she'd have dinner with the three of them, she said, but sometimes her plans would change and they'd have to substitute lunch for dinner.

Gisela couldn't come to the funeral. She was in Argentina for the year, working with the architectural firm that Mr. DeCuervo's father had started.

After all the mourners left, Mr. DeCuervo gave us a sympathy note from Gisela, with a beautiful pen-and-ink of our mother inside it. The two men went into the living room and took out a bottle of Scotch and two glasses. It was like we weren't there; they put on Billie Holiday singing "Embraceable You," and they got down to serious drinking and grieving. Lizzie and I went into the kitchen and decided to eat everything sweet that people had brought over: brownies, strudel, pfeffernuesse, sweet potato pie, Mrs. Ellis's chocolate cake with chocolate mousse in the middle. We laid out two plates and two mugs of milk and got to it.

Lizzie said, "You know, when I was home in April, he called every day." She jerked her head toward the living room.

I couldn't tell if she approved or disapproved, and I didn't know what I thought about it either.

"She called him Bolivar."

"What? She always called him Gaucho, and so we didn't call him anything."

"I know, but she called him Bolivar. I heard her talking to him every fucking day, El, she called him Bolivar."

Tears were running down Lizzie's face, and I wished my mother was there to pat her soft fuzzy hair and keep her from choking on her tears. I held her hand across the table, still holding my fork in my other hand. I could feel my mother looking at me, smiling and narrowing her eyes a little, the way she did when I was balking. I dropped the fork onto my plate and went over and hugged Lizzie, who leaned into me as though her spine had collapsed.

"I asked her about it after the third call," she said into my shoulder.

"What'd she say?" I straightened Lizzie up so I could hear her.

"She said, 'Of course he calls at noon. He knows that's when I'm feeling strongest.' And I told her that's not what I meant, that I hadn't known they were so close."

"You said that?"

"Yeah. And she said, 'Honey, nobody loves me more than Bolivar.'

And I didn't know what to say, so I just sat there feeling like 'Do I really want to hear this?' and then she fell asleep."

"So what do you think?"

"I don't know. I was getting ready to ask her again—"

"You're amazing, Lizzie," I interrupted. She really is, she's so quiet, but she goes and has conversations I can't even imagine having.

"But I didn't have to ask because she brought it up herself, the next day after he called. She got off the phone, looking just so exhausted, she was sweating but she was smiling. She was staring out at the crab apple trees in the yard, and she said, 'There were apple trees in bloom when I met Bolivar, and the trees were right where the sculpture needed to be in the courtyard, and so he offered to get rid of the trees and I said that seemed arrogant and he said that they'd replant them. So I said, "Okay," and he said, "What's so bad about arrogance?" And the first time he and Daddy met, the two of them drank Scotch and watched soccer while I made dinner. And then they washed up, just like at the cabin. And when the two of them are in the room together and you two girls are with us, I know that I am living in a state of grace.'"

"She said that? She said 'in a state of grace'? Mommy said that?"

"Yes, Ellen. Christ, what do you think, I'm making up interesting deathbed statements?" Lizzie hates to be interrupted, especially by me.

"Sorry. Go on."

"Anyway, we were talking and I sort of asked what were we actually talking about. I mean, close friends or very close friends, and she just laughed. You know how she'd look at us like she knew exactly where we were going when we said we were going to a friend's house for the afternoon but we were really going to drink Boone's Farm and skinny-dip at the quarry? Well, she looked just like that and she took my hand. Her hand was so light, El. And she said that the three of them loved each other, each differently, and that they were both amazing men, each special, each deserving love and appreciation. She said that she thought Daddy was the most wonderful husband a woman could have and that she was very glad we had him as a father And I asked her how she could do it, love them both, and how they could stand it. And she said, 'Love is not a pie, honey. I love you and Ellen differently because you are different people, wonderful people, but not at all the same. And so who I am with each of you is different, unique to us. I don't choose between you. And it's the same way with Daddy and Bolivar. People think that it can't be that way, but it can. You just have to find the right people.' And then she shut her eyes for the afternoon. Your eyes are bugging out, El."

"Well, Jesus, I guess so. I mean, I knew …"

"You knew? And you didn't tell me?"

"You were eight or something, Lizzie, what was I supposed to say? I didn't even know what I knew then."

"So, what did you know?" Lizzie was very serious. It was a real breach of our rules not to share inside dirt about our parents, especially our mother; we were always trying to figure her out.

I didn't know how to tell her about the three of them; that was even less normal than her having an affair with Mr. DeCuervo with Daddy's permission. I couldn't even think of the words to describe what I had seen, so I just said, "I saw Mommy and Mr. DeCuervo kissing one night after we were in bed."

"Really? Where was Daddy?"

"I don't know. But wherever he was, obviously he knew what was going on. I mean, that's what Mommy was telling you, right? That Daddy knew and that it was okay with him."

"Yeah. Jesus."

I went back to my chair and sat down. We were halfway through the strudel when the two men came in. They were drunk but not incoherent. They just weren't their normal selves, but I guess we weren't either, with our eyes puffy and red and all this destroyed food around us.

"Beautiful girls," Mr. DeCuervo said to my father. They were hanging in the doorway, one on each side.

"They are, they really are. And smart, couldn't find smarter girls."

My father went on and on about how smart we were. Lizzie and I just looked at each other, embarrassed but not displeased.

"Ellen has Lila's mouth," Mr. DeCuervo said. "You have your mother's mouth, with the right side going up a little more than the left. Exquisite."

My father was nodding his head, like this was the greatest truth ever told. And Daddy turned to Lizzie and said, "And you have your mother's eyes. Since the day you were born and I looked right into them, I thought, 'My God, she's got Lila's eyes, but blue, not green.'"

And Mr. DeCuervo was nodding away, of course. I wondered if they were going to do a complete autopsy, but they stopped.

My father came over to the table and put one hand on each of us. "You girls made your mother incredibly happy. There was nothing she ever created that gave her more pride and joy than you two. And she thought that you were both so special …" He started crying, and Mr. DeCuervo put an arm around his waist and picked up for him.

"She did, she had two big pictures of you in her studio, nothing else. And you know, she expected us all to grieve, but you know how much she wanted you to enjoy, too. To enjoy everything, every meal, every drink, every sunrise, every kiss …" He started crying too.

"We're gonna lie down for a while, girls. Maybe later we'll have dinner or something." My father kissed us both, wet and rough, and the two of them went down the hall.

Lizzie and I looked at each other again.

"Wanna get drunk?" I said.

"No, I don't think so. I guess I'll go lie down for a while too, unless you want company." She looked like she was about to sleep standing up, so I shook my head. I was planning on calling John anyway.

Lizzie came over and hugged me, hard, and I hugged her back and brushed the chocolate crumbs out of her hair.

Sitting alone in the kitchen, I thought about John, about telling him about my mother and her affair and how the two men were sacked out in my parents' bed, probably snoring. And I could hear John's silence and I knew that he would think my father must not have really loved my mother if he'd let her go with another man; or that my mother must have been a real bitch, forcing my father to tolerate an affair "right in his own home," John would think, maybe even say. I thought I ought to call him before I got myself completely enraged over a conversation that hadn't taken place. Lizzie would say I was projecting anyway.

I called, and John was very sweet, asking how I was feeling, how the memorial service had gone, how my father was. And I told him all that and then I knew I couldn't tell him the rest and that I couldn't marry a man I couldn't tell this story to.

"I'm so sorry, Ellen," he said. "You must be very upset. What a difficult day for you."

I realize that was a perfectly normal response, it just was all wrong for me. I didn't come from a normal family, I wasn't ready to get normal.

I felt terrible, hurting John, but I couldn't marry him just because I didn't want to hurt him, so I said, "And that's not the worst of it, John. I can't marry you, I really can't. I know this is pretty hard to listen to over the phone. ..." I couldn't think what else to say.

"Ellen, let's talk about this when you get back to Boston. I know what kind of a strain you must be under. I had the feeling that you were unhappy about some of Mother's ideas. We can work something out when you get back."

"I know you think this is because of my mother's death, and it is, but not the way you think. John, I just can't marry you. I'm not going to wear your mother's dress and I'm not going to marry you and I'm very sorry."

He was quiet for a long time, and then he said, "I don't understand, Ellen. We've already ordered the invitations." And I knew that I was right. If he had said, "Fuck this, I'm coming to see you tonight," or even, "I don't know what you're talking about, but I want to marry you anyway," I'd probably have changed my mind before I got off the phone. But as it was, I said good-bye sort of quietly and hung up.

It was like two funerals in one day. I sat at the table, poking the cake into little shapes and then knocking them over. My mother would have sent me out for a walk. I'd started clearing the stuff away when my father and Mr. DeCuervo appeared, looking more together.

"How about some gin rummy, El?" my father said.

"If you're up for it," said Mr. DeCuervo.

"Okay," I said. "I just broke up with John Wescott."

"Oh?"

I couldn't tell which one spoke.

"I told him that I didn't think we'd make each other happy."

Which was what I had meant to say.

My father hugged me and said, "I'm sorry that it's hard for you. You did the right thing." Then he turned to Mr. DeCuervo and said, "Did she know how to call them, or what? Your mother knew that you weren't going to marry that guy."

"She was almost always right, Dan."

"Almost always, not quite," said my father, and the two of them laughed at some private joke and shook hands like a pair of old boxers.

"So, you deal," my father said, leaning back in his chair.

"Penny a point," said Mr. DeCuervo.

The Battle-Field

Phyllis Bottome

Everyone said: "What a sweet dear girl Madeline Writtle is! What a pity that she is so delicate!"

Her delicacy made Madeline look a great deal younger than she was, and prevented her from doing things that she sometimes thought she would have liked to do, and sometimes knew that she would not.

She was the apple of her mother's eye.

As the years slipped nonchalantly past her, Madeline grew more and more sweet and dear; and more and more delicate.

Finally she became definitely ill.

Her mother nursed her night and day with unexampled fortitude and skill. Madeline had the best advice, and at least half a dozen expensive treatments for diseases from which, it turned out afterwards, she had never suffered.

At last her mother heard that at Davos there was a specially good sanatorium, run by a young English "genius". Roughly speaking, Hugh Potter had not got genius, but he had an unusual amount of common-sense.

All sorts and kinds of lung patients were under his charge; some of them became a great deal better, and some of them were actually cured.

Of course occasionally some of them died; but then consumptive patients will do this anywhere, if they are not careful; and sometimes even if they are.

From the first, Madeline liked the look of Dr. Hugh Potter. He was lean and hatchet-faced, and had kind grey eyes, which did not look particularly hard at her.

Madeline had been examined by dozens of doctors. She made no kind of fuss at having her blood tested, nor did she mind her arm being crushed in an india-rubber band, in order to have her blood pressure examined; and when she was being stethoscoped, she coughed discreetly, and not in the doctor's face.

After she had been X-rayed and sounded with the utmost thoroughness, Dr. Potter led her back into his sunny office, and made her sit in a particularly easy chair opposite his desk.

Madeline was by now very exhausted, but too interested to show it. She had a feeling that this time she really was going to find out what was the matter with her.

Dr. Potter asked her none of the usual questions. Instead, he offered her a cigarette, and lit one of his own. His speculative, unaggressive eyes gazed past her out of the window.

"What do you think yourself," he asked at last, "that you are suffering from?"

To Madeline's surprise, she found herself speaking the truth. This was not a habit of hers, because the truth is often painful to others; and sometimes to oneself. No sweet dear girl can ever afford any great indulgence in candour, and Madeline, when she was feeling despondent, automatically lied.

"I don't know what is the matter with me!" she exclaimed. "I sometimes think nothing is! I mind this worst of all. It makes me feel so guilty and extravagant! When doctors say I am a little run down—or it is only nerves—I cry my eyes out; for if this is all it is— and it makes me feel so deadly ill—how can I ever get any better? I am not just tired and sick of everything, I feel sick of being ill too! If I can't get better, I should like to die!"

Dr. Potter listened to this outburst with sympathetic attention. "When you say you feel sick of everything," he asked her, "does it include 'everybody'—or any particular person?"

Madeline hesitated. "People tire me so," she answered; "except Mother—Mother's wonderful!"

She drew a deep breath and began to tell Dr. Potter all about her mother. This made her forget that she was tired. Very few grown-up daughters ever had such a perfect maternal relationship; and Madeline, with a flushed face and brilliantly sparkling eyes, poured out a striking picture of their miraculously harmonious tie. She had always admired her mother. She could scarcely remember her father, who died of lung trouble after a long and terrible illness. Her mother had nursed him with unflinching care and affection, but there was from the first no hope. Mrs. Writtle was left a young and attractive widow with two little girls, Madeline and her elder sister Caroline.

Caroline was a very strong character, and both Madeline and her mother leaned on Caroline; but Madeline had sometimes wished that her elder sister were a shade less powerful.

Caroline, with ruthless unselfishness, did everything for Madeline and her mother. In spite of her home cares Caroline's school work was brilliant. She had a voice like a nightingale; and out of a long list of devoted admirers, whom she alternately attracted and repelled, Caroline became engaged to a particularly nice young man called "George".

And then Caroline was drowned, in a swimming race, in the open sea. The sea became extremely rough; all the other competitors turned back, but Caroline swam on. Her mother and Madeline saw her drown before their eyes. They were quite helpless, of course, and George, who had an inveterate dislike of swimming-races, was not there.

Mrs. Writtle had become for several months completely

incapacitated, and Madeline and George (Caroline's devoted fiancé) had had a dreadful, but somehow or other rather stimulating, time looking after her.

A fresh catastrophe, of a very different though equally painful nature, heralded the recovery of Mrs. Writtle. George, although he was broken-hearted, developed an ungratifying passion for Madeline's mother.

In the end—since he quite refused to get over it—they had to give George up.

This had been a great shock to them both, for by now they had come to lean on George.

Madeline began to be definitely ill, instead of merely very delicate, and had gone on being ill ever since.

Madeline found it rather odd telling Dr. Potter this long story, because it seemed to have nothing to do with her lungs, but somehow or other, prompted by a few unaggressive but intelligent questions, the story of her life came out.

When Madeline had quite finished, and let George go—as she had let him go in real life—with a pang half of relief and half of direst agony, Dr. Potter remained for several minutes restfully silent. Madeline stared unseeingly at the golden peaks which faced the sanatorium across the narrow valley.

The beauty of the peaks did not mean anything to Madeline. No beauty had meant anything to her since her mother had said, "I am never going to see George again!" with a noble gesture of complete renunciation, which had included Madeline.

"You have something the matter with your lungs," Dr. Potter said at last. "But you can get over it, you know. You needn't feel a fraud. It is quite definite; but people have had more the matter with them than you have, and yet got better, and people have had less, and succeeded in dying of it. You see there is quite a wide margin of choice in these matters.

"I think if you do exactly what I tell you, and have confidence in my power to help you, you can get well; but I should like to be sure of your loyal co-operation before I undertake your case. Will you tell me quite truthfully—what you really feel about it?"

"What I feel about—what?" Madeline asked him, with a startled sensation at the pit of her stomach. "I don't quite understand what you mean. I always do what my doctors tell me. Mother will tell you I am considered a very good patient."

"What do you feel about getting well?" Dr. Potter gently persisted. "You see, you can be a good patient, and yet not be what I consider a good case.

"When I undertake a case, I want to know that the patient really wants to get well!

"Patients aren't ill because they want to be. There is no easy solution—like Christian Science—in the scientific world. But behind the organic trouble which has come upon the patient, perhaps from infection or exposure, perhaps from some more subtle and less easily ascertainable cause, there lies sometimes a very definite obstacle to recovery—the aim of the patient to escape through his illness—from a position which has become intolerable to him.

"We all have a private goal, sometimes it is a secret even from ourselves; but it is part of a doctor's business to find out what his patient's goal is—before the illness can be successfully dealt with."

Madeline thought this over very carefully. She was an intelligent woman, though she had not always found it convenient to use her intelligence. She began to wonder for the first time whether she did really want to get quite well? What would she do if recovery were granted to her?

She was thirty-five and did not intend to marry. Nor did she have any career to take up again. She had always been nice about religion, but not enthusiastic. She and her mother liked reading out loud. Their favourite books were usually about the love affairs of kings' mistresses. They referred to them as "Historical Memoirs", and felt that these dubious researches were quite above ordinary novels. But even if Madeline remained ill, they could still read out loud, or at any rate her mother could still read out loud to Madeline.

Madeline said emphatically after a long reflective pause: "Of course I want to get well! It would be such an intense relief to Mother if I were! It's too awful to think what she's been through—and I can't bear having to go on torturing her!"

"Well, then," said Dr. Potter, with a charming smile, in which, however, there was something a little quizzical, "we'll try it out. But I shall want the whole of your active co-operation. To begin with, I am afraid that you must come into the sanatorium for a time. Your mother can remain in Davos if she wishes, but we don't allow relations to stay in the sanatorium with the patients. We have our own nurses."

Madeline stared at him in blank incredulity. "But Mother"—she began—"is such a perfect nurse! No trained nurse can touch her. Nobody else has ever done things for me. We've never once been parted. We aren't rich at all—but we have enough to stay on here together; and Mother, I know, has never dreamed of leaving me—she'll be—we couldn't—I don't think you understand—!"

Madeline broke off breathless, gazing at Dr. Potter with helpless entreaty. He met her gaze with courteous inflexibility.

"It isn't," he said gently, "a question of money or of your mother's capacity to nurse you. She can come in every day to see you in the visiting hours. We have very generous ones. From ten to twelve, from four to six in the afternoons, and from eight to ten in the evenings; so it is practically the whole day, you see, and the intervening hours are those in which we wish the patient to be alone and not to speak. This is one of the points in which you must have sufficient confidence in me. If you do not have it, I should not advise you to become my patient!"

Madeline's eyes dropped to the floor. She felt that it would be restful to trust him. He seemed able to let her confide in him, without in any way getting the better of her by his knowledge. She felt, too, that it wasn't for himself—it was for her sake that he wanted to know the truth of her being.

This hidden goal that he had spoken of was a secret to Madeline; but she suddenly knew that she wanted to find the secret out, and that she was willing for Dr. Potter to help her to find it.

She already liked him enough to want to like him more. But her liking for Dr. Potter was that of a drowning man for a straw; it would not lead, she knew, to anything like that irritated agony which she had once felt for George.

About that cruel business she had always been wholly silent; and she was silent now. It had made never seeing George again like cutting the heart out of her body. But such a wildly beating heart that she had felt at the time—perhaps she would get on better without it.

How wonderful her mother had been, never to have cared for George, or if she cared for him, decently, as a woman over forty should care for a dead daughter's fiancé, how fine of her to have pushed this affection aside, so that she could give her undivided heart to her living daughter! Madeline and her mother were all in all to each other.

No other man could ever now perturb their sacred relationship.

Madeline said, after a long pause: "Perhaps we can explain to Mother—but there must be no question of my having in any way to desert her. I couldn't do that, you know. I shouldn't get better if I had to bear the burden of any pain I was causing her."

Dr. Potter said quickly: "It needn't appear like that, I think. I'd like to talk to her now—if I may. You're very tired I can see. May I ring for Nurse to take you into the lounge and give you tea? Or, if you've quite decided to stay on with us, she might take you up to your room at once. We could telephone for your luggage later."

"But I can't decide without asking Mother!" Madeline expostulated. "How can I? It is just what I mean I mustn't do! It would seem like deciding against her. I can't do that!"

Madeline looked up at him uneasily. Fear cramped her heart. How disappointed she would be if her mother refused to let her go into the sanatorium! And yet how could they expect her mother not to refuse when the plan involved their virtual separation? Madeline could not press for it, when (unless she seemed to hate it, too) her mother might suffer an unpardonable betrayal.

"If I were you," said Dr. Potter gravely, "I would decide now— by myself. I will explain to your mother anything that you wish explained. Your best interest must be, I feel sure, what she most desires."

"Yes—oh, yes!" moaned Madeline. She could not admit, even to Dr. Potter, that her mother's belief in Madeline's best interest would never involve any withdrawal from her own inexorable maternal care. "But I must just ask her—Dr. Potter!" Madeline feebly murmured. "I can't let it seem to be a decision arrived at away from her."

"But I think you can," Dr. Potter urged, still very gently. "You are of an age to make such a decision for yourself, and I should strongly advise you to make it now, Miss Writtle. If you leave it until you have seen your mother, you may find it much more difficult to press. Whereas, if you take for granted that she would want what is a necessary part of your cure, you will be helping her to accept this separation much more easily."

Waves of heat and cold passed in turn over Madeline's sensitive body. Did she want—or did she not want—this sudden cleavage? How disloyal the word "separation" sounded, and how cruel the loneliness which she was enforcing upon her mother's heart, as well as upon her own! She knew, if she once saw her mother's pained, devoted eyes and heard her gentle voice saying, "But, my darling— we shouldn't be together!" everything but blank surrender to her mother's wishes would be impossible. Did she want to make this surrender, after all? Or did she wish to stay in the sanatorium by herself?

"Oh, please—I can't bear it!" she whispered.

Dr. Potter got up at once. "You wish me to fetch your mother, then?" he asked in a voice studiously devoid of any pressure—even of encouragement.

"No! Not my mother!" Madeline heard herself gasp. Anguish swallowed her; but at the bottom of her anguish she felt a strange relief.

Dr. Potter rang a bell at his elbow, and a smiling young woman came to the door. "Nurse Mitchell," he said, "this is Miss Writtle, our new patient. Please take her up to No. 24, and make her comfortable. I should like her to have some tea immediately."

Then he turned back to Madeline. "I'll explain everything to your mother," he said, and as she looked into the impersonal kindliness of his eyes, the feeling of relief deepened.

The strangest part of the whole thing was that Mrs. Writtle seemed unaware of any conflict having been necessary. From the first she took the sanatorium for granted. When Madeline said, "It's so dreadful, darling, to think of being here by myself—and your having to be in some horrible place alone!" her mother had said: "Ah, but you see, dearest, it's all part of the cure. Lung patients have to be in sanatoriums—and one quite understands doctors not wanting relations! One has only to think of what some relations are! I quite like my little hotel. It's only a stone's throw away. I can see your windows."

It was but another proof of her mother's courage and patience. Madeline felt with crushed humility how still more wonderful her mother was, and how dreadful it was of her not to mind that, wonderful or not, she was—at any rate—a stone's throw away!

When Madeline woke in the morning, even after a bad night, and she generally had bad ones, she felt a strange sense of refreshment and peace.

She liked her large, light room, with practically nothing in it but air and light.

She could look from her bed, through wide-open windows, straight into the sky. Her eyes lost themselves in the blueness of great distances.

She did not want to have her bed taken out onto the balcony—that felt somehow exposed and tiring. The sun was too strong a companion for her brittle strength. She wanted just to lie in her room, and let the sweet, keen air pour over her, not to have to speak or smile, or say: "I'm better today, darling!" when she wasn't! She felt an unutterable relief.

By the time her mother came, the worst of the morning was already over. Madeline had been washed and had had her breakfast; and got over the reaction from the bad night which followed so soon upon the first relief of day. She knew that when it was twelve o'clock she would be alone again. Once more Madeline could close her eyes and feel as if the blueness of the distance had swallowed her vexed consciousness into its serene unconsciousness.

Hour after hour slipped by in uninterrupted peace. At one o'clock Nurse would come in with a joke and a smile, and all manner of little dishes on a tray, which were to tempt Madeline to eat. She came back again just before two, but Nurse did not say anything, or look at all grieved, when the tray—very little emptier—had to be carried out again.

Just at first, Madeline felt the early afternoon hours a burden. She grew bored and restless. Fever started up and made her apprehensive and rudderless. She found herself longing for her mother's watchful tenderness. But after a week or two Madeline hardly noticed the daily rise of temperature. A new quietness stole into her being. She noticed, instead, the pine trees, and watched the slow, friendly light pass from branch to branch, interrupted sometimes by the bright flash of a bird's wing, or the friendly scuttle of a leaping squirrel.

Madeline felt the silence sink, deeper and deeper, into her separate heart. Her mother did not come to see her after the tea hours were over; and when she had left her, the red light outside Madeline's door sprang on, and Dr. Potter came in, later than he visited his other patients. He used to stay quite a long time with Madeline, ten minutes always, sometimes a quarter of an hour. She did not know if she liked their strange talks, but she knew that she lived on them.

He always knew how she was, without her having to tell him. He did not praise her, nor find her heroism touching, as most doctors did, for as far as pain and physical discomfort were concerned, Madeline was a heroine. He seemed, instead, to turn away from the struggle of her outer being, and to attack a citadel which she had never even known she was defending. Sometimes he laughed at her a little, but only when he could make her laugh at herself with him; and he pointed out to her ways in which she could get the better of what had once seemed to Madeline her virtues.

Her symptoms he listened to, if she made him, but he did not seem to attach much importance to them.

Madeline did not go on making Dr. Potter listen. She let everything go, except what he put into her hands.

He asked her to let one of the other patients look in for a minute or two after supper, nor did he seem to mind if Madeline found it tiring.

The patient he suggested her seeing was a girl called Clara; other patients came, too, sometimes, but Madeline hardly counted them as her real visitors. It was true, they told her intimate things about themselves—their troubles and their joys. Madeline gave them her full attention, she looked at them with her soft kind eyes as if she liked them. She never judged people, she wanted to let them off from all their difficulties, even from their crimes. She never had advice for them—only appreciation for whatever they had decided to do; and the sanatorium patients found her—as everybody had always found her—wonderfully sweet and dear. But Clara was different—she seemed to penetrate below the surface of Madeline's ready sympathy. Madeline found that she sometimes said to Clara things that she really meant.

Her mother noticed at once that Clara's visits tired Madeline.

She did not approve of any of Madeline's visitors; and indeed Madeline herself sometimes felt that people stayed too long and had too many troubles; but Madeline had not felt these drawbacks to Clara's visits.

When Madeline told Dr. Potter that her mother felt that she was seeing too many visitors, he said,

"Do you talk a great deal to your mother?"

"In a way, I do," Madeline admitted, "but, you see, anyone one knows so well isn't tiring! It's not like a conversation. You lie quite still, and just say whatever comes into your head to say—or you don't talk at all—Mother's just there—in my mind—if you know what I mean?"

Dr. Potter knew what Madeline meant, but he did not agree with her. He shook his head laughingly. "Don't you sometimes think that's a lazy way of living?" he asked her. "You can hardly make your mind work at all if the other mind you live with is so accessible to yours. And your mind must work or it loses grip—your body, too, if things are made too easy for it, that loses grip as well. You can't separate body and mind."

Madeline left this to think about when he'd gone. She used to spend half her wakeful nights thinking over what Dr. Potter had said to her, and trying to practise it. She would talk to her mother about these things in the mornings, but her mother did not find that Dr. Potter was always right. She liked him, but she thought he hardly knew what was good for Madeline as well as she herself did.

Even in the most perfectly run sanatoriums things do go wrong.

A meal once in a while was incorrectly ordered, a nurse once or twice forgot a medicine. These were things which, when Mrs. Writtle herself was nursing Madeline, could not conceivably have happened; but Dr. Potter never took these lapses as much to heart as Mrs. Writtle felt he should have taken them.

"Your mother thinks you sacred," Dr. Potter pointed out to Madeline. "Personally I think it's rather better that you shouldn't be nursed so splendidly. You'll get to feel more like other people if you have to rough it a little, and not quite so remote like a Madonna in a shrine."

"In a shrine," Madeline said, rather puzzled; "of course I'm not at all like a Madonna—but what do you mean by a shrine?"

"Well, your mother thinks your ill-health is a kind of shrine," Dr. Potter ventured after a brief pause. "We look upon illness here as a thing to get rid of. I fancy your mother rather venerates it for itself."

"It's only that she's so anxious," Madeline told him, rather reprovingly.

"Yes—yes, of course!" Dr. Potter agreed hurriedly. "That's the worst of devotion—its trade-mark is anxiety!"

"Don't you believe in being fond of people?" Madeline demanded; and it seemed to her as if her whole life was at stake, and in danger of being overturned. For what had she ever done but be fond of people? Her mother—Caroline—George—Clara! Was the entire accumulation of her years to be flung onto a rubbish heap by this young iconoclast?

"Well, of course, it depends on what you mean by 'fond'," Dr. Potter admitted. "No one can help taking more pleasure in one human being rather than in another. But the test of affection is behaviour. If we behave rightly to anyone, we are fond enough—and if we're as it were too fond, we don't always behave rightly. We slacken the fibres of their hearts and our own into the bargain. That's not the prettiest kind of devotion, is it?"

"What a very curious idea!" said Madeline, which was from her almost as violent a repulse as if she had boxed Dr. Potter's ears.

However, he did not seem to mind having his ears boxed. One day he even asked Madeline what had happened to George, though he must have known that George was not a subject that she wished touched upon.

Madeline drew a quick breath of displeasure, but in the end she told Dr. Potter George's name, and even where he lived, and what his work was; and that he had never married. George had always been faithful to Caroline's—and her mother's—memories.

Then Dr. Potter took up the subject of Clara. "Your mother," he said, "tells me that her visits are very bad for you—and that you never see her without a rise of temperature and a bad night following. I rather wonder why that is?"

Madeline sighed deeply. "Perhaps Mother is right," she admitted reluctantly. "I love seeing Clara, and I find her so interesting that perhaps it takes it out of me. But, Dr. Potter, what is it in me for—if it's not ever to be taken out? I think I'd rather go on being tired and just seeing Clara!"

"Perhaps," Dr. Potter suggested, "it would be better if she came to see you earlier in the day. Say tea-time, instead of after dinner?"

"But she can't do that!" Madeline said quickly; "that's Mother's time!"

Thinking it over afterwards, Madeline wondered if it had not been the beginning of the trouble. Clara continued to drop in, and her mother continued not to like it. She saw that Clara's visits were doing Madeline more harm, and she expostulated with Madeline as well as with Dr. Potter.

Madeline said that Dr. Potter must settle whom she could see and whom she couldn't see; and her mother, after a strange cold pause, asked: "Why? Hitherto you have considered me the best judge of what was good for you. After all, I've nursed you on and off for thirty-six years—and Dr. Potter has known you in a much more superficial way and only for a few months."

This seemed unanswerable, and Madeline merely flushed painfully and grew that night more feverish than ever.

There was no doubt that Madeline was rapidly becoming worse. She suffered from blinding headaches. Her temperature ran up and up. She slept less; and the trays went down emptier and emptier.

Even Madeline herself at last did not want Clara to come.

One day Dr. Potter came into Madeline's room, and sat there for a long time without speaking. They knew each other so well by now that she did not feel afraid of his silence. She knew that it was being spent on her. He was thinking of some way to stop her pain or to get the fever down.

"Madeline," he said at last, "do you remember our first talk together—do you trust me?"

She roused herself to look straight at him. "More than anyone in the world," she said, and then, with a faint smile, she added: "Except Mother, of course."

"I think that I want you to trust me rather more than that," Dr. Potter said quietly. "I want you to trust me as a human mind which has centred itself in the study of how to fight your disease—I do really know more about it than your mother, who loves you, and is sometimes deflected by her devotion from the knowledge of what is best for you."

"Well—yes"—agreed Madeline—"I think I do—in that way—trust you even more! I hope it is not disloyal of me—and I wouldn't want Mother to know it—but I expect I do trust you more. I do think you know better what is good for me."

"Well, that's very satisfactory if you do think that," Dr. Potter said gravely, "because I am going to put you to the test. I do not want your mother to stay up in Davos any longer. You see too much of her. You get too absorbed in her anxiety for you. She is a point of conflict, and you are not strong enough for conflict. I want you to be here quite alone. I want you to have a being that is separate from your mother's. At first I thought we might manage this without sending your mother away; but I see that it is impossible, you lean on her too much. You can't, as people say, 'exist without her'. Well—that's no existence at all which is wholly dependent on the company of another human being. You would really enjoy her more if you were less dependent on her. She shuts you out from the circle of your own contemporaries. You cannot afford to let her do this. They—or she—must go! And for the moment they are better for you than she is. I must ask you to try to believe this and to strengthen my hand by agreeing to let her go. This must be a deep agreement on your part, Madeline. You mustn't just say, 'Yes, Dr. Potter,' and then lie here, crushed, and die on my hands. You must agree to get well, and to be happier alone."

"To be happier alone—!" Madeline closed her burning eyes. She was always happier alone. She did not have to be divided then, to belong half to her mother, in whose being she felt the roots of her own; or pulled away from her by Dr. Potter and Clara into a new and sparkling life, with elements of sheer terror, just at a moment when she hardly felt enough of her old life left not to crumble into a bleak eternity.

Madeline herself knew that she was not getting well. Sometimes she would wake and feel Death in the room. She would remember George with the old agony and unrest; and think of her mother with a new agony and unrest—longing to live for her, longing to die, to be away from her. But how could she agree with Dr. Potter and send her mother from her, as if she were dismissing a faulty housemaid? Her mother, who was so fine and exquisite a personality—so unruffled and quiet a nurse, so devoted and perfect a comrade? What did age matter, when they were both at one?

She opened her eyes and looked at Dr. Potter. "Do you want me to break my mother's heart?" she asked, in a voice so harsh that she hardly recognized it for her own.

"That is an expression," Dr. Potter said coldly, "which is more picturesque than solid. It is usually employed when a depressing feeling has to be faced, either by oneself or another person. To tell the truth, I expect your mother will feel more angry than broken-hearted; and the person she will be angry with—will be me! She may be a little shocked at your agreeing to follow my advice. However, you are too ill for her to say very much about it to you; and I don't mind her being angry—once I have convinced myself that you won't get better *with* her—and will get better *without* her."

Madeline was silent for a long time. She tried to master her thoughts, but they kept revolving in her flustered mind. Her heart pounded against her side, like heavy seas against the side of a waterlogged boat. George kept coming into her mind. George being sent away so bravely, so self-sacrificingly—and with such an air of being got rid of for everybody's good all round. Even at the time, she had not wanted George to be sent away, and she had known that George hadn't wanted to go. But he had gone, of course. And now her mother was being sent away from her too—against her will, and half against her heart. She said to herself sternly: "What a coward I must be—to have to be so protected! And always to hurt most those I care for most!"

She had not known that she spoke aloud until Dr. Potter answered her. "Well, yes—perhaps rather a coward," he said pleasantly, "but as you grow stronger, you'll get over that. It's not, you know, altogether your fault that you are a coward. You've been brought up to be nice—and that's a dangerous profession. It's rather sapped your courage, here and there. You'll find that it will come back to you, once you've learned to be alone. That's the first step. Are you going to take it?"

Madeline did not hesitate at all now. She said; "Yes, I'm going to take it. Tell Mother what you like—!"

But after Dr. Potter had left her, she remembered that she would have to see her mother before she went.

Her mother's reddened eyelids and her quivering lips said all she could not say to Madeline. Madeline's stricken heart clamoured back: "I am killing her—why am I killing her?"

Suddenly Mrs. Writtle's fortitude broke down. She leaned over Madeline and cried: "Why are you sending me away from you—dearest?"

This was more than Madeline could bear. She cried out: "Mother—oh, Mother! Don't leave me! I don't want you to go away!" A taste as bitter as salt was in her mouth. Suddenly something swelled up quite softly in her throat, and poured out over her hands and on the sheets, in a bright scarlet flood. Madeline saw a strange expression on her mother's face, a sort of excitement—like a justified prophet, seeing the city he loves and is banished from, destroyed by fire from on high. Madeline suddenly remembered what to do—she pushed a little red bell close to her—Dr. Potter had told her only yesterday that in three minutes after she rang it—from wherever he was in the sanatorium—he could reach her room. After she had pressed it, she stared helplessly at the terrible scarlet flood. It wasn't hurting her—that was something. But if it came any faster, it would choke her. Still she wasn't frightened. It was as if a Power, in spite of herself, had come to her assistance. She wouldn't have to stay with her mother; nor would her mother have to leave her.

The door opened, and Nurse was there—and Sister, following swiftly at her heels—and then Dr. Potter's face. Not at all tragic, but rather concentrated.

"We'll soon put a stop to this," he said cheerfully.

And quite soon the haemorrhage stopped. Her mother was not there any more. Sister seemed to mind most about the sheets, but very soon the whole room was white and spotless again—and Dr. Potter smiled down at Madeline and said:

"Don't try to talk. If you want anything, you can whisper. Nurse will stay with you for a bit. I want you to suck this ice, and then you can go to sleep! I'll see about your mother."

So Madeline sucked ice, and slept; and when she woke up, they told her, her mother had gone.

Madeline had frightful headaches for a week afterwards, and could neither write nor read letters—but after that she began to feel slightly better. And one day Clara slipped into the room again.

Clara gave Madeline a fresh cool feeling, as if a nymph had come to visit her out of a stream. Clara was as cool and quiet as a snowdrop—and yet her thin face, with its black bands of hair round it, and lips with the side-ways smile, expressed the sort of fun a very ill person can safely enjoy.

Madeline loved seeing Clara. She told her how awful it was not having her mother. "You see," Madeline said, "all the time—half of me is her loneliness." But she did not say that the other half of her was relief.

Clara looked grave and full of sympathy, but after a little while she began to talk about the Schatz Alp instead. She had just been out for her first walk. It was astounding how much better Madeline began to feel.

The weeks slipped past her.

She sat up to have her bed made. She was allowed to wash herself. She sat up for tea. She liked lying out on the balcony now, and looking down over Davos. So large, and busy, and alive—and at dusk, its lights shone like a field of stars beneath her feet. And at last Madeline put her clothes on. Clara had made her like her clothes—and together they walked—a wonderful hundred yards into a blue sun-soaked pine wood; and Madeline knew that she was alive again.

"Now," she thought to herself, "Mother ought to come back." And then she felt that she was trembling, from having walked so far, and all the blue went out of the sky and the fir scent from the pines.

Clara's frightened eyes made Madeline pull herself together; but after she had got back to her room in safety, she felt that she did not want to go for a walk again.

One day, while Madeline was on her balcony alone, after tea, enjoying the sunset, Nurse came in and said, "Would you like to see a visitor?"

Madeline said, "Yes, of course," thinking it was Clara. But it was not Clara, she heard a man's step instead, and said to herself, "Oh, bother! I suppose this is the new assistant—not Dr. Potter!" She thought it a little unkind of Dr. Potter not to come himself. And then suddenly she heard a voice say, "Madeline!" and looking up, she saw George's face.

The air broke into a mist.

George did not look ten years older, but he had lost his slender, touching adolescence, which had once matched her own. He was more solid now, but the same George with the same delightful friendly smile, which started in his eyes and then travelled slowly downward to his rather heavy lips.

George explained that he'd been skiing in the neighbourhood—he'd met Potter—and Potter had asked him his name—and then told him that a friend of his was at the sanatorium—and wouldn't mind if he popped in.

"You're all right, aren't you?" George demanded, breaking off his explanation rather suddenly. "You look too stunning for words! I hope you don't mind my having turned up. But it seemed silly, when we were so near each other not to look in."

Madeline found her voice at last, the mist cleared away from George's face, and she said: "Yes, it would have been silly not to look in." After all, it wasn't Madeline whom he shouldn't see again—it was only her mother.

He told Madeline that he was staying at a village halfway between Davos and Klosters. But he did not go on staying at it very much, for the next two weeks he was at the sanatorium every day. He took Madeline out for walks, for sleigh rides, and every day to some new place for tea.

Madeline wondered if she ought to stop him; but she did not even write to tell her mother that George was there, or that the question of stopping George had again cropped up in a new form. For Madeline saw that George was in love with her. Perhaps he was in love with them all three—with Caroline in her grave—with her mother in her sacrificial banishment—and with Madeline in her illness. George had always had a tenderness for handicapped or broken creatures.

He seemed, at any rate, blissfully happy, and if he had come to ski—it was not skiing that was making him happy.

At last he said to Madeline, not at all in a frightening way, but as if he was explaining something about which they already knew a good deal: "Of course I'm still in love with you, you know!"

"Oh, but I'm old and ill!" cried Madeline quickly. "Besides, you never were—it wasn't me you were in love with—then."

"Funnily enough, you look a great deal younger," said George, "and yet more like—well, more like your mother—if you know what I mean. I always did admire your mother!"

"It is ten years ago," said Madeline steadily, "and she doesn't look so very much older now. She's still quite beautiful, George—and far more useful than I am. No wonder that you always admired her!"

George looked slightly uncomfortable. "Well, yes—I dare say she is," he admitted; "still, you know, I can't quite forgive her. She needn't have packed me off for ever. I hadn't been married to Caroline—so even if that ridiculous law hadn't been changed—I wasn't your deceased sister's husband, was I?"

"That hadn't anything to do with it, though," Madeline said rather shortly, "seeing it wasn't me—" She stopped abruptly. Something in George's eyes stopped her.

"Oh, yes it was!" George said, with great firmness; "of course it was! Who else could it have been? Your mother said it would kill you to know about it. And of course you were most awfully delicate—I knew that. And you'd been so wrapped up in Caroline. And so was I, for the matter of that. But it's no use not getting over things, is it?"

Madeline opened her lips to speak, and then shut them again. Everything in her heart stood still and turned to ice. Her mother had lied to her. George had never loved her mother! Her mother had told Madeline that George loved her, in order to put Madeline off George. Perhaps her mother had loved George herself, but much more likely she had loved Madeline! This was the love from which Madeline had so nearly died! But for the sake of this love Madeline felt that she must shield her mother from George—she must shield her mother from everyone—except herself.

"No!" Madeline said at last, drawing a long deep breath which seemed to blow away half her life. "No, George—I don't think it's ever any use—not getting over things!"

I Stand Here Ironing

Tillie Olsen

I stand here ironing, and what you asked me moves tormented back and forth with the iron.

"I wish you would manage the time to come in and talk with me about your daughter. I'm sure you can help me understand her. She's a youngster who needs help and whom I'm deeply interested in helping."

"Who needs help." Even if I came, what good would it do? You think because I am her mother I have a key, or that in some way you could use me as a key? She has lived for nineteen years. There is all that life that has happened outside of me, beyond me.

And when is there time to remember, to sift, to weigh, to estimate, to total? I will start and there will be an interruption and I will have to gather it all together again. Or I will become engulfed with all I did or did not do, with what should have been and what cannot be helped.

She was a beautiful baby. The first and only one of our five that was beautiful at birth. You do not guess how new and uneasy her tenancy in her now-loveliness. You did not know her all those years she was thought homely, or see her poring over her baby pictures, making me tell her over and over how beautiful she had been—and would be, I would tell her—and was now, to the seeing eye. But the seeing eyes were few or non-existent. Including mine.

I nursed her. They feel that's important nowadays. I nursed all the children, but with her, with all the fierce rigidity of first motherhood, I did like the books then said. Though her cries battered me to trembling and my breasts ached with swollenness, I waited till the clock decreed.

Why do I put that first? I do not even know if it matters, or if it explains anything.

She was a beautiful baby. She blew shining bubbles of sound. She loved motion, loved light, loved colour and music and textures. She would lie on the floor in her blue overalls patting the surface so hard in ecstasy her hands and feet would blur. She was a miracle to me, but when she was eight months old I had to leave her daytimes with the woman downstairs to whom she was no miracle at all, for I worked or looked for work and for Emily's father, who "could no longer endure" (he wrote in his good-bye note) "sharing want with us."

I was nineteen. It was the pre-relief, pre-WPA world of the depression. I would start running as soon as I got off the streetcar, running up the stairs, the place smelling sour, and awake or asleep to startle awake, when she saw me she would break into a clogged weeping that could not be comforted, a weeping I can yet hear.

After a while I found a job hashing at night so I could be with her days, and it was better. But it came to where I had to bring her to his family and leave her.

It took a long time to raise the money for her fare back. Then she got chicken pox and I had to wait longer. When she finally came, I hardly knew her, walking quick and nervous like her father, looking like her father, thin, and dressed in a shoddy red that yellowed her skin and glared at the pock marks. All the baby loveliness gone.

She was two. Old enough for nursery school they said, and I did not know then what I know now—the fatigue of the long day, and the lacerations of group life in nurseries that are only parking places for children.

Except that it would have made no difference if I had known. It was the only place there was. It was the only way we could be together, the only way I could hold a job.

And even without knowing, I knew. I knew the teacher that was evil because all these years it has curdled into my memory, the little boy hunched in the corner, her rasp, "why aren't you outside, because Alvin hits you? that's no reason, go out, scaredy." I knew Emily hated it even if she did not clutch and implore "don't go Mommy" like the other children, mornings.

She always had a reason why we should stay home. Momma, you look sick. Momma, I feel sick. Momma, the teachers aren't there today, they're sick. Momma, we can't go, there was a fire there last night. Momma, it's a holiday today, no school, they told me.

But never a direct protest, never rebellion. I think of our others in their three-, four-year-oldness—the explosions, the tempers, the denunciations, the demands—and I feel suddenly ill. I put the iron down. What in me demanded that goodness in her? And what was the cost, the cost to her of such goodness?

The old man living in the back once said in his gentle way: "You should smile at Emily more when you look at her." What *was* in my face when I looked at her? I loved her. There were all the acts of love.

It was only with the others I remembered what he said, and it was the face of joy, and not of care or tightness or worry I turned to them—too late for Emily. She does not smile easily, let alone almost always as her brothers and sisters do. Her face is closed and sombre, but when she wants, how fluid. You must have seen it in her pantomimes, you spoke of her rare gift for comedy on the stage that rouses a laughter out of the audience so dear they applaud and applaud and do not want to let her go.

Where does it come from, that comedy? There was none of it in her when she came back to me that second time, after I had had to send her away again. She had a new daddy now to learn to love, and I think perhaps it was a better time. Except when we left her alone nights, telling ourselves she was old enough.

"Can't you go some other time, Mommy, like tomorrow?" she would ask. "Will it be just a little while you'll be gone? Do you promise?"

The time we came back, the front door open, the clock on the floor in the hall. She rigid awake. "It wasn't just a little while. I didn't cry. Three times I called you, just three times, and then I ran downstairs to open the door so you could come faster. The clock talked loud. I threw it away, it scared me what it talked."

She said the clock talked loud again that night I went to the hospital to have Susan. She was delirious with the fever that comes before red measles, but she was fully conscious all the week I was gone and the week after we were home when she could not come near the new baby or me.

She did not get well. She stayed skeleton thin, not wanting to eat, and night after night she had nightmares. She would call for me, and I would rouse from exhaustion to sleepily call back: "You're all right, darling, go to sleep, it's just a dream," and if she still called, in a sterner voice, "now go to sleep, Emily, there's nothing to hurt you." Twice, only twice, when I had to get up for Susan anyhow, I went in to sit with her.

Now when it is too late (as if she would let me hold and comfort her like I do the others) I get up and go to her at once at her moan or restless stirring. "Are you awake, Emily? Can I get you something, dear?" And the answer is always the same: "No, I'm all right, go back to sleep, Mother."

They persuaded me at the clinic to send her away to a convalescent home in the country where "she can have the kind of food and care you can't manage for her, and you'll be free to concentrate on the new baby." They still send children to that place. I see pictures on the society page of sleek young women planning affairs to raise money for it, or dancing at the affairs, or decorating Easter eggs or filling Christmas stockings for the children.

They never have a picture of the children so I do not know if the girls still wear those gigantic red bows and the ravaged looks on the every other Sunday when parents can come to visit "unless otherwise notified"—as we were notified the first six weeks.

Oh it is a handsome place, green lawns and tall trees and fluted flower beds. High up on the balconies of each cottage the children stand, the girls in their red bows and white dresses, the boys in white suits and giant red ties. The parents stand below shrieking up to be heard and the children shriek down to be heard, and between them the invisible wall "Not To Be Contaminated by Parental Germs or Physical Affection."

There was a tiny girl who always stood hand in hand with Emily. Her parents never came. One visit she was gone. "They moved her to Rose Cottage," Emily shouted in explanation. "They don't like you to love anybody here."

She wrote once a week, the laboured writing of a seven-year-old. "I am fine. How is the baby. If I write my leter nicly I will have a star. Love." There never was a star. We wrote every other day, letters she could never hold or keep but only hear read—once. "We simply do not have room for children to keep any personal possessions," they patiently explained when we pieced one Sunday's shrieking together to plead how much it would mean to Emily, who loved so to keep things, to be allowed to keep her letters and cards.

Each visit she looked frailer. "She isn't eating," they told us.

(They had runny eggs for breakfast or mush with lumps, Emily said later, I'd hold it in my mouth and not swallow. Nothing ever tasted good, just when they had chicken.)

It took us eight months to get her released home, and only the fact that she gained back so little of her seven lost pounds convinced the social worker.

I used to try to hold and love her after she came back, but her body would stay stiff, and after a while she'd push away. She ate little. Food sickened her, and I think much of life too. Oh she had physical lightness and brightness, twinkling by on skates, bouncing like a ball up and down up and down over the jump rope, skimming over the hill; but these were momentary.

She fretted about her appearance, thin and dark and foreign-looking at a time when every little girl was supposed to look or thought she should look a chubby blonde replica of Shirley Temple. The door-bell sometimes rang for her, but no one seemed to come and play in the house or be a best friend. Maybe because we moved so much.

There was a boy she loved painfully through two school semesters. Months later she told me how she had taken pennies from my purse to buy him candy. "Liquorice was his favourite and I brought him some every day, but he still liked Jennifer better'n me. Why, Mommy?" The kind of question for which there is no answer.

School was a worry to her. She was not glib or quick in a world where glibness and quickness were easily confused with ability to learn. To her overworked and exasperated teachers she was an overconscientious "slow learner" who kept trying to catch up and was absent entirely too often.

I let her be absent, though sometimes the illness was imaginary. How different from my now-strictness about attendance with the others. I wasn't working. We had a new baby, I was home anyhow. Sometimes, after Susan grew old enough, I would keep her home from school, too, to have them all together.

Mostly Emily had asthma, and her breathing, harsh and laboured, would fill the house with a curiously tranquil sound. I would bring the two old dresser mirrors and her boxes of collections to her bed. She would select beads and single ear-rings, bottle tops and shells, dried flowers and pebbles, old postcards and scraps, all sorts of oddments; then she and Susan would play Kingdom, setting up landscapes and furniture, peopling them with action.

Those were the only times of peaceful companionship between her and Susan. I have edged away from it, that poisonous feeling between them, that terrible balancing of hurts and needs I had to do between the two, and did so badly, those earlier years.

Oh there are conflicts between the others too, each one human, needing, demanding, hurting, taking—but only between Emily and Susan, no, Emily toward Susan that corroding resentment. It seems so obvious on the surface, yet it is not obvious. Susan, the second child, Susan, golden- and curly-haired and chubby, quick and articulate and assured, everything in appearance and manner Emily was not; Susan, not able to resist Emily's precious things, losing or sometimes clumsily breaking them; Susan telling jokes and riddles to company for applause while Emily sat silent (to say to me later: that was *my* riddle, Mother, I told it to Susan); Susan, who for all the five years' difference in age was just a year behind Emily in developing physically.

I am glad for that slow physical development that widened the difference between her and her contemporaries, though she suffered over it. She was too vulnerable for that terrible world of youthful competition, of preening and parading, of constant measuring of yourself against every other, of envy, "If I had that copper hair," or "If I had that skin ..." She tormented herself enough about not looking like the others, there was enough of the unsureness, the having to be conscious of words before you speak, the constant caring—what are they thinking of me? What kind of an impression am I making?— there was enough without having it all magnified by the merciless physical drives.

Ronnie is calling. He is wet and I change him. It is rare there is such a cry now. That time of motherhood is almost behind me when the ear is not one's own but must always be racked and listening for the child cry, the child call. We sit for a while and I hold him, looking out over the city spread in charcoal with its soft aisles of light. "*Shoogily*," he breathes and curls closer. I carry him back to bed, asleep. *Shoogily*. A funny word, a family word, inherited from Emily, invented by her to say: *comfort*.

In this and other ways she leaves her seal, I say aloud. And startle at my saying it. What do I mean? What did I start to gather together, to try and make coherent? I was at the terrible, growing years. War years. I do not remember them well. I was working, there were four smaller ones now, there was not time for her. She had to help be a mother, and housekeeper, and shopper. She had to set her seal. Mornings of crisis and near hysteria trying to get lunches packed, hair combed, coats and shoes found, everyone to school or Child Care on time, the baby ready for transportation. And always the paper scribbled on by a smaller one, the book looked at by Susan then mislaid, the homework not done. Running out to that huge school where she was one, she was lost, she was a drop; suffering over the unpreparedness, stammering and unsure in her classes.

There was so little time left at night after the kids were bedded down. She would struggle over books, always eating (it was in those years she developed her enormous appetite that is legendary in our family) and I would be ironing, or preparing food for the next day, or writing V-mail to Bill, or tending the baby. Sometimes, to make me laugh, or out of her despair, she would imitate happenings or types at school.

I think I said once: "Why don't you do something like this in the school amateur show?" One morning she phoned me at work, hardly understandable through the weeping: "Mother, I did it. I won, I won; they gave me first prize; they clapped and clapped and wouldn't let me go."

Now suddenly she was Somebody, and as imprisoned in her difference as she had been in anonymity.

She began to be asked to perform at other high schools, even in colleges, then at city and state-wide affairs. The first one we went to, I only recognized her that first moment when thin, shy, she almost drowned herself into the curtains. Then: Was this Emily? The control, the command, the convulsing and deadly clowning, the spell, then the roaring, stamping audience, unwilling to let this rare and precious laughter out of their lives.

Afterwards: You ought to do something about her with a gift like that—but without money or knowing how, what does one do? We have left it all to her, and the gift has as often eddied inside, clogged and clotted, as been used and growing.

She is coming. She runs up the stairs two at a time with her light graceful step, and I know she is happy tonight. Whatever it was that occasioned your call did not happen today.

"Aren't you ever going to finish the ironing, Mother? Whistler painted his mother in a rocker. I'd have to paint mine standing over an ironing-board." This is one of her communicative nights and she tells me everything and nothing as she fixes herself a plate of food out of the icebox.

She is so lovely. Why did you want me to come in at all? Why were you concerned? She will find her way.

She starts up the stairs to bed. "Don't get me up with the rest in the morning." "But I thought you were having midterms." "Oh, those," she comes back in, kisses me, and says quite lightly, "in a couple of years when we'll all be atom-dead they won't matter a bit."

She has said it before. She *believes* it. But because I have been dredging the past, and all that compounds a human being is so heavy and meaningful in me, I cannot endure it tonight.

I will never total it all. I will never come in to say: She was a child seldom smiled at. Her father left me before she was a year old. I had to work her first six years when there was work, or I sent her home to his relatives. There were years she had care she hated. She was dark and thin and foreign-looking in a world where the prestige went to blondeness and curly hair and dimples, she was slow where glibness was prized. She was a child of anxious, not proud, love. We were poor and could not afford for her the soil of easy growth. I was a young mother, I was a distracted mother. There were the other children pushing up, demanding. Her younger sister seemed all that she was not. There were years she did not want me to touch her. She kept too much in herself, her life was such she had to keep too much in herself. My wisdom came too late. She has much to her and probably nothing will come of it. She is a child of her age, of depression, of war, of fear.

Let her be. So all that is in her will not bloom—but in how many does it? There is still enough left to live by. Only help her to know—help make it so there is cause for her to know that she is more than this dress on the ironing-board, helpless before the iron.

The Stepmother

Mary Arden

If no one ever called Esther King beautiful—and however infatuated they were they really couldn't have—her little nose was too pointed, her cheekbones too high—at least no one ever questioned her looks—picked them to pieces—thought of her as either pretty or plain. No, not even her enemies, and she had quite a lot of enemies sprinkled about among her schoolgirl adorers.

"Whatever you can see in that old Miss King, Fanny, simply beats me, you know. She's not a patch on Miss Henderson. She's not even jolly or—or anything like that," said Ernestine. She felt in a lazy after-lunch mood, so she pulled up her legs and sprawled, half sitting, half lying, on her bed at the corner of the dormitory.

"Oh, but Ernie," said Frances from the next-door bed, "she's so—" her grey eyes became dreamy, she clasped her knees tighter with her hands, she put her chin down on to her knees, "she's so—fascinating. When she looks at me I feel as if everything was sort of melting inside me, and if she told me to go right off that very second and fetch her something from the North Pole—I would. I'd go right off that very minute."

"Oh," groaned Ernestine, "you're getting sloppy. You've been getting worse and worse all this last week." Suddenly she sat up straight and looked quite fierce.

"I hate her," she said, "I hate her! How dare she make you get sloppy!"

"No, no, *no*, Ernie. Oh, don't! I'm not a bit, really and truly. I love her frightfully—that's all. If only you'd see what I *mean* about her!"

"I see her every day of my life, and that's enough, isn't it?"

"Oh, no, it isn't. Not if you keep feeling furious; not if—"

Slowly, gradually the door opened. A smiling face looked round, a coaxing, yet half-laughing voice said:

"You're talking secrets, you two, *I* know."

Ernestine tilted her little square chin defiantly. Frances looked away and grew slowly, painfully red, and as if it were somehow part of a dance, Miss King tripped lightly into the room.

"A-a-ah!" she said, indicating Frances with a little white hand that lifted itself slowly and as though unwillingly into the air. "A-a-ah! She's blushing! Come, what is it all about? What were you talking about when I looked in, eh?"

She came, half tripping, half gliding, over to Frances, gently tugged a lock of her hair, then let that languid little hand pass slowly down her cheek, and so under her chin and raised her face.

Ernestine pulled her legs up on to the bed again and looked on scornfully. Frances' big eyes were very tortured.

"Oh, well," said Miss King, laughing down at her, "you needn't *really* tell me, dear, because I know. You were talking about me."

Oh, how guilty Frances felt, how miserable, how disloyal!

"But never mind, dear," and actually, yes, actually, she stooped and gave her adorer a quick kiss on the cheek. Then she fluttered away.

"Sneaky old thing," said Ernestine almost before the door was shut, "to go listening at keyholes the way she does!"

"Ernestine!"

"Oh, you needn't look so shocked," said Ernestine, with a toss of the head. "She does, and I don't care if she hears me say so, either."

But nothing that Ernestine could say would ever make any real difference to Frances. No one would ever be able to persuade her that her Miss King was not absolute perfection.

But why did her feeling torture her so frightfully? She was unhappy when she was away from her, but when she was with her she could never make the most of the opportunity. She felt dumb and awkward. If Miss King kissed her it was bliss. But one kiss was always only a beginning. She wanted more—more.

Sitting at the long table for meals she was conscious only of Miss King who sat at the foot. She felt her there. Somehow she didn't want to look at her, but she knew she would have to. No, she would *not* look. Yes, she would have to. She raised her head and stared, fascinated.

And what special thing it was that drew her so she had no idea. She didn't even wonder. The little hands that moved, that lifted, the way she had of talking with her head a little on one side—her nose, her chin. Everything was part of the whole, and all was fascinating.

Now she had seen her looking.

Ah! Miss King's glance shot down the table. As usual, it stabbed, it tortured. Frances blushed so terribly that the roots of her hair began to tingle.

"Frances, will you send the jam up, please?" said the mocking voice. "Goodness, how the child is blushing! Look at her, girls! Whatever can be the matter?"

Ten pairs of eyes stared at Frances. She wanted fearfully to sink through the floor. But for Miss King to say things like that only coiled the strands of the web tighter and tighter.

And at night she lay in bed and listened to the other girls giggling and whispering, and thought, "Why doesn't Miss King come up and say good night? What a long time she is!"

She could hear talk and laughter going on in the mistress's room downstairs. She kept her eyes glued to the crack of light that showed under the door.

Now! A door opened, banged shut. There were steps on the stairs. Now was her moment.

When Miss King came to her bed she gave her a strangling hug.

"Come, come, dear, don't pull my head off!"

But it was all nothing but moments, flashes. There were such heaps of things she wanted to talk to her about that she felt she would never be able to.

For one thing, Miss King always wore an emerald ring on the third finger of her left hand. How awfully Frances wanted to ask her about it—to know all about *him*—what he was like—were they going to be married soon? But, of course, it was out of the question. She would never be able to. Never.

And then there came one marvellous evening.

It was very cold. Everywhere was draughty. Frances was so frozen that she couldn't do her prep., and she knew she had a cold coming because her throat felt so frightfully sore. At supper she couldn't swallow a thing.

She must have looked awfully miserable, for just as she was going out of the dining-room, Miss King came and put a hand on her shoulder.

"Why, what's the matter, my child? You look wretched. And how cold you are! Come up to my room till bedtime. I've got a little stove up there, you know. I'm cold, too. We can both get warm."

Miss King sat in the basket arm-chair, and Frances on the floor beside her. The light was not lit. The stove was warm and comforting. It made a very nice yellow glow.

Miss King let her hand fall and remain as if lifeless over Frances' shoulder. Frances put up her hand and stroked Miss King's fingers. (Wonderful that, though they said nothing, she should feel that she was so much more intimate with Miss King than she had ever been before!) Very daring, she began to play with the emerald ring.

Still they said nothing. At last Frances asked, almost whispering: "Have you been engaged for a very long while now, Miss King?"

No answer. She glanced cautiously up.

Her mistress lay quite still in the basket-chair. Her other arm was curled above her head. But she couldn't be annoyed; she hadn't taken her hand away.

"Yes," said Miss King, and her voice sounded awfully sad, "I've been engaged for a very long while now, dear." A breathless pause. "He died of heart-failure," she said, "four years ago."

How tragic! What a secret for Frances to know! She was not going to tell anyone about it. Not Ernestine. She felt it would be wrong to use Miss King's tragedy for making Ernestine see what kind of person she really was. No, she would keep her knowledge absolutely to herself. She adored her mistress more than ever.

So that no one was so simply amazed as Frances when next term Miss King came back *engaged*—really engaged to someone alive. Oh, she couldn't believe it—it was simply too astonishing for words, but, of course, it must be *all right*—she knew that.

Other people—though not, of course, in the same way—were amazed too.

Why should they be amazed? Miss King didn't like it. How unflattering it was!

"My *dear*," said Miss Harris, the games mistress, when she heard the news. "*No!*" She stood before the fire in the mistress's room, her hands on her hips, her large feet planted wide apart on the rug. The dusty black velvet band she wore over her hair was a little bit crooked as usual. "Well, this *is* a surprise," said she, and the pale, short-sighted science mistress poked her head round the *Morning Post* and gaped like a fish.

Miss King laughed and tossed her head. "You'd made up your minds I was going to be an old maid, I suppose." It would have been delicious to add, "like the rest of you."

"Oh, *no*," said Miss Harris, taking her in slowly from head to feet and then from feet to head, "not *at all*, and *why* I should be so surprised I *can't* imagine." Suddenly a little thrill ran down Esther King's spine. They were jealous. How too delicious!

Engaged! The news went simply flying all over the school, and when on Saturday afternoon, someone—a *man*—appeared to escort Miss King into the town, all the walls had eyes.

Here were the two coming out into the hall.

How lovely Miss King looked, thought her adorers, in her grey furry hat and her furry collar, and her cheeks quite pink—but he wasn't half good enough for her. "All she could get, of course," said her enemies. But the adorers quelled them with terrible looks.

He had a large round red face, beaming and good-natured, large hands, a bald pate, red, pendulous ears that were covered at the tips with very fine white down, a curving belly, a watch-chain. He spoke in a loud, confident, benevolent voice. He called Miss King "My dear," as if they'd been man and wife for years.

But Miss King liked that. Independence and so forth were all very well—but it gave a woman such a sense of fitness to be owned—to feel herself overshadowed by his large benevolent bulk.

And as she sat pouring out his tea for him in the nice, select little tea-shop, where there were chintz curtains, shaded lights, a violin, a 'cello and a piano making soft music in the background, and where even the tinkling of the cups and saucers was subdued and very pleasant to hear, she watched with infinite satisfaction his large hand with the signet ring on it fold round the cup, grasp it, lift it, leaving the handle unused on the other side. How like a man it was not to use the handle!

"Ah!" he drank deep. "That's a becoming hat," he said. "Suits you very well, my dear."

"Oh, do you think so?" Miss King looked pleased and animated. She even blushed just a little, like the quite young girl she was not.

"I do," said the confident voice.

How it boomed! How it surrounded! Miss King felt that she was, so to speak, flying on the wings of that voice, out of her old self into a different one, out of her old life into a new.

But somehow she never quite realized how complete had been her flight until she came to rest as Mrs. Andrew Mellaby in the large, awe-inspiring bedroom at Richmond.

"Do you think it's all right?" said Andrew, waving a comprehensive hand to include the light oak wardrobe with huge heavy doors, the bedstead with brass knobs and snow-white quilt, the dressing-table with all its mirrors and a little glass vase standing on it that was stuffed very tight with speckled sweet-williams.

"Oh, *quite,* dear; I think it's very nice indeed," said she, hoping that no note of doubt had come creeping into her voice. But when she thought of it, how like Andrew it all was! Though why one should think that ... The former Mrs. Mellaby, on whom, for some reason, Esther had never allowed her thoughts to dwell, must have had a say in the furniture after all. Could she—Esther—possibly alter it all—very gradually—by degrees, so as not to hurt his feelings? The sense that all must be representative of *her*—the other—was so very depressing.

Why had she not come to the house before they were married? She felt that terrific, drastic alterations would have been so much easier before—well, to be quite honest with herself—before she had lost her freedom. "No, no, I don't want to go through the door of my new home until after we are married," she had told him a little breathlessly. Why? Had she been putting off—the loss of her freedom? No, surely not! What a ridiculous idea!

"Dear house!" she told herself persuasively. "Dear room, so exactly like Andrew—so almost naive like him!" And yes, it *was*—even down to the little vase of squashed-in sweet-williams. If Andrew had not only that moment come into the house she would have believed he had put it there with his own hands.

As it was, of course, he couldn't have. It must be that rather formidable cook-housekeeper person in the tight black dress she had seen downstairs. She would have to be very careful how she dealt with her. It might turn out that it was best to dismiss her altogether,

"Tired, dear?" said Andrew. "You're looking a shade down, I fancy." He took her small hand between his two large, cushiony ones and gave it a slow pat. "You want your *tea!*" he said, speaking as if out of deep wells of knowledge.

"Oh, yes, I *do* want my tea," said Esther, and she took her hat off with a tired gesture that was like a sigh, and going over to the large gleaming mirror, she tilted it down a little, and patted and smoothed her dark hair and tucked away a few wisps under the plaited coils she wore over her ears.

Tea was laid in Andrew's little upstairs study.

"Oh, but in future we must certainly have tea in the drawing-room or garden," thought Esther, "and oh, dear me, this bread and butter is far too thick, and I detest these solid home-made cakes, and this china is so abominably thick and coarse—I really must get it relegated to the kitchen."

"Nice to be home again," said Andrew, surveying with an approving eye his shelves stacked with very solidly bound editions, his solid desk with the revolving chair in front of it, the sheepskin rug, the long group photograph over the mantelpiece that included himself, his partner and all their subordinates.

"How do you think you're going to like it, my dear?" said he, turning on her the full glory of his confident smile.

"Oh, of course I shall like it, dear, of course I shall," said Esther, and boldly she bit into the bread and butter. "Naturally though," she went on because she wished to be *quite* candid, "I shall have to find my footing—to—er—to realize. I mean—it's all so new, you know, so—"

"Ah, yes," he nodded reflectively, "and you haven't met Ella yet, have you?"

Ella! Her pulse gave a little quick jump. Good heavens, no! Of course, Ella was—a big consideration.

"No, and I'm simply longing to see her, dear." She looked down, half smiling. "I'm simply longing to see my new friend—my—little sister." She lowered her voice. "I think that's the right relationship, don't you? Not mother and daughter, but—sisters." She leant forward. Lightly, gracefully her hand fell on to his knee, with a candid girlish expression she looked up into his face; she said, meeting his eyes, "Dear, I shall love her, I know."

Ella was expected back from Paris a week later.

On the day when she was due to arrive Esther bustled about the house putting little extra touches here and there that she thought Ella might notice and like. She put flowers in Ella's bedroom, and a little velvet cat with pins stuck into him and a large pale blue ribbon tied to his tail, now squatted on the dressing-table. She had already changed the cushion-covers in the drawing-room and had bought a new charming tea-set. But tea—that splendid aid to the making of friends—would be out of the question on this first afternoon. Ella would not arrive till seven o'clock.

Long before the clock struck Esther was prepared. With her hair carefully done and wearing a pretty, fussy afternoon frock, she flitted about like a butterfly, never staying in any place for more than a moment at a time. No one to see her but the stolid cook-housekeeper, and the new startled-looking parlourmaid. If her former adorers could have seen Esther, how they would have blushed, half turned away, hardly dared to look! It gave her a little flutter to imagine them, but now as never before she was out to conquer—*this* should be love at first sight.

Tring! What a loud, confident ring at the bell. Was it *her*, or was it Andrew coming home early? Esther hovered in the drawing-room. It was simply absurd, but her heart was beating quite fast.

Yes, it was *her*.

Esther could hear her saying a few words to the parlourmaid. Her voice sounded confident and gay. Then the door opened.

In came a tallish graceful girl in a neat grey travelling suit—fair hair showing from under her hat, a charming half-open mouth.

Before she had a chance to do anything or speak, Esther ran lightly up to her, put a hand on her shoulder and looked into her face.

Her skin was very clear and fine. Somehow Esther couldn't be quite sure whether the colour in her cheeks was really there or whether it was just a sort of reflection of light. She bent forward. (Oh, shades of the adorers!) She gave her a quick kiss on the forehead. "My *dear*!" she said.

Ella twitched an eyebrow. She gave herself a little shake. "We haven't really said how-do-you-do yet, have we?"

Dear me, how stupid! How—idiotic!

"No, I suppose we haven't really," said Esther, laughing, and retreating a little, she held out her hand.

Ella grasped it firmly. "I think I'll just run up and take my things off, first, shall I?"

Should Esther go with her? No, she thought not.

"Oh, yes, you must be fearfully tired and hot, poor child. I'll put some chairs out under the trees. We don't have supper till eight—or would you like to have something to eat now?"

"No, no, thanks very much. I had tea and a bun or two at the station."

Esther heard her whistle on the stairs.

What a queer, abrupt child it was! Oh, well, motherless, of course. What was her impression? Odd—she had always made up her mind at once before, but now, for some reason, she didn't *want* to. Why?

She arranged deck-chairs on the lawn. Then she lay back and lit a cigarette. She felt that she must look very graceful and attractive lying there. But uncomfortable and disconcerting though it was, when Ella came leisurely across the grass in a plain blue-striped cotton frock, Esther felt quite overdressed with her lacy sleeves and fussiness at the neck. Absurd! There was no dressing for dinner nowadays because Andrew didn't like it, but, goodness me, it was afternoon! Esther was really being very silly—she must have got quite unnerved.

"Have a cigarette!"

She held out her silver cigarette-case, and Ella took one—a little condescendingly, Esther felt. Then Esther began to ask questions.

Did you have a nice journey? Is it good to be in England again? Were you happy in Paris? Were the other girls nice?

To all of which Ella answered—politely.

Then she changed on to a more intimate note.

"I *do* hope we are going to be happy together, Ella!"

"Oh, yes," said Ella cheerfully, "I expect so."

But not content with this, Esther bent forward and said very earnestly, "I think we are going to love each other—somehow."

"M'm. Oh, yes, quite likely."

False move. Fancy Esther making a false move! What was the matter with her? What queer effect was this child having upon her?

What, indeed?

In the days, in the weeks after Ella's coming, Esther was not at all happy. She felt that she was always trying to be nice to Ella, and yet always her advances were met—no, not exactly coldly, and yet somehow not *met* at all. And still—utterly unlike the Miss King of former days—Esther simply had to go on being sweet to this obstinate creature who refused to respond to her charms. Sometimes she hated herself for it, sometimes there came a little twinge of hatred for Ella, but there was something about the child ... Oh, wait a while and she would succeed. Having patience was dreadfully humiliating, but still. ...

And coming down one morning to breakfast she found a letter from Frances waiting for her.

"My darling Miss King," cried the letter, "please will you not mind if this is rather nonsense. I am writing it after prep. and my head has all gone funny. But I must tell you. I can't help it. I do *miss* you so. ..." Defiantly Esther looked up at Ella who was eating her eggs and bacon with the appetite of a young and desperately healthy creature.

The letter gave Esther a sense of power. It was like suddenly receiving a whole fresh supply of ammunition. If only she could have a talk with Ella *now*! But no, she wouldn't be able to. As soon as Andrew had wiped the egg off his lips, swallowed the last of his coffee, cleared his throat and gone off to put on his city-going boots, Ella got up and went out too.

Of course the child would be out all the morning. She was *always* going out; often for the whole day—sometimes for supper. Esther felt that she was distant, separate. Who were her friends? What did she do? Surely it was a mother's—or, in this case she would call it an elder sister's place to find out.

At any rate, Ella would be in to lunch for once.

Esther waited until lunch was over, and then, when they had gone into the drawing-room and the door was shut and she had handed Ella a cigarette, she said:

"I am wondering why you don't ask your friends to the house, dear, I feel your life is absolutely separate and apart. Actually I don't know what you do or who you know."

Ella flung herself down on the sofa and just looked.

"And after all I don't know why I shouldn't," said Esther, a little bit crossly.

"Well," said Ella, "I don't quite know either, except that of course they're *my* friends, aren't they? You might not like them. ... Wouldn't Father's friends be rather more in your line?"

Father's friends, indeed! Esther had seen enough of them. Stuffy married old bores or golf-playing club men.

"But, Ella, I—I don't know quite why you should say that. Does it mean you think I'm so frightfully ancient, or what?" Esther looked down and from where she stood by the mantelpiece, slowly drew her cigarette along the edge.

Those dreadfully candid eyes regarded her doubtfully.

"No, no. No, I didn't exactly mean I thought you were *old*. ..."

Ye gods! But this was too much! A little fire began to burn in Esther's bosom, but whatever happened she was going to seem quite cool.

"All the same," she said, "I don't see why you shouldn't ask them to the house, dear. How can you tell what I shall think of them—or—what they will think of me, for that matter, until we've seen each other?"

"No," said Ella reflectively. "No, of course."

"Then why don't you ask them?" said Esther, as if she were scoring a point.

But suddenly, disconcertingly—it seemed as if all the things she did were disconcerting—Ella jumped up from the sofa.

"Oh, I don't really know why," she said. She walked away, she opened the door, she turned to say over her shoulder, "It's just that somehow I *don't want to*—that's all."

How exasperating! But Esther was not exactly angry. No, she was still too bent on her conquest for that. She thought calmly.

She went to the little rosewood desk in the corner and took out a sheet of rough-edged note-paper. She wrote quickly:

"Dear little Frances,—

"Very many thanks for your letter. I should be delighted if you could come and spend part of your holidays with me. Will your people let you? Tell them—"

and so, and so on.

There! There was a brilliant idea. Ella should *see*! It wouldn't be long now, either. There was only a fortnight now to the holidays at most....

And with almost as much trepidation and hope as she had waited for the coming of Ella she now waited for the coming of Frances.

As for Ella, so for Frances, she made careful preparation. Flowers in her room, tentative remarks to Ella. "Please be very nice to the child, dear. She's a sweet little thing. You'll like her, I know."

As for Ella, so for Frances, she wore her prettiest frock on the day of her expected arrival. But this time she went to meet her guest, and walked up and down the platform impatient—yes, quite impatient—swinging to and fro her closed parasol.

How late she was! She had been walking up and down there at least a quarter of an hour. But, of course, with these metropolitan trains there never was any exact time.

Ah, at last! Another train. Surely this must be the one!

Grinding and grating on the lines the train slowed down. The doors slid open. Two unhurrying women were disgorged, and behind them—yes, that child behind them was Frances.

Flushed and excited she leapt out on to the platform. She ran up to Esther.

"Here I am, Miss King! Here I am!" And at once, wonder of wonders, instead of a pat on the cheek, a quick kiss, a handshake, immediately she was enfolded in a long, warm, scented embrace.

"Oh, Miss King, I *am* pleased to see you!"

"I'm pleased to see you too, my child. Come along. Is that all you've got—a suit-case? Let me carry it. It isn't far."

"Oh, no, Miss King. You mustn't. I couldn't let you carry it. Let me."

Esther laughed—laughed merrily.

"All right then, I won't. We'll have half each." And with Frances' hand touching Miss King's on the handle of the suit-case they came out into the sun.

Up the road, round the corner.

"Now, just one more turn, and there we are," Esther encouraged her gaily. How gay Miss King was! Frances felt she was being treated absolutely as an equal—not as a schoolgirl any more.

"There! Now the next drive to this is ours!"

The big house slept in its sheltering garden. Like eyelids the green blinds were closed. A gardener was mowing the tennis lawn round at the side of the house. Faintly from the drive you could catch the scent of cut grass. But everything was very quiet, and as they went into the dark hall, it seemed cool, dim and silent as a cave. Ella and Andrew would not be home till evening. Esther was glad that she would have the child to herself.

Over the little *tête-à-tête* tea under the trees, she felt herself glow in the warmth of Frances' adoration. It was strange how she craved that adoration to-day—bathed in it, encouraged it with every word and gesture.

"Oh, Miss King," said Frances shyly, "are you very happy here? We miss you awfully at school."

"Yes, my child," said Esther, "I—am very happy."

"You have a stepdaughter, haven't you, Miss King?" said Frances, nervously playing with the hem of her dress.

"Yes, dear, I have."

"And is she very—very nice?"

"Yes, she is very nice," said Esther a little hurriedly, and quickly she added, "but she is a strange person. You mustn't mind if she is a little bit abrupt at first. Of course, it is such a long time since she has had a mother. I don't know what it is. ... Sometimes it seems as if she has a little fire inside her. ... She *never* lets it break out, dear. She is always—calm. Perhaps if she *did* let it. ... Oh, no, I don't know why I'm describing her to you like this. You'll be getting a bad impression. She is very, very pretty, dear, and she's charming."

"Oh, do tell me what she is like to look at!"

But Esther didn't seem to want to talk about Ella any more just then, so Frances had just to wait and see.

And in the evening she came. She arrived by the same train down from town as Andrew. She held out her hand stiffly to Frances. "How-do-you-do?" she said, looking at her with her calm, penetrating glance. "It was a hot day for travelling, wasn't it?"

"Yes," said Frances, childishly digging the toe of her shoe into the ground, "it was a bit." She felt rather awkward, rather dumb. But she liked this beautiful stepdaughter of Miss King's awfully. Oh, she liked her very much indeed.

"Well, little girl!" said Mr. Mellaby. He came and patted her on the head. He did make her feel dreadfully young—but then, of course, he was so old—a kind of grandfather.

Already it was beginning to be twilight, so that half-way through supper it was time to light the lamps.

Up went the lights. The dining-room changed, and in a circle of warm orange lamplight sat the four.

The french windows were open to the garden. Outside it was nearly dark. It was still. No one spoke. Yet to Esther it seemed that the silence was not of constraint—rather was it more like a silence of understanding. But no, not exactly that—no one was necessarily conscious as she was of strange, inevitable harmony. Inevitable. Yes. All was so. The two girls. Their shining hair. The fair one and the sleek mouse-colour. Frances' soft, quick alertness, her eager, loving glances. Ella's beautiful hand lifting the silver cream-jug, the little ring that gleamed on her finger. Never had Ella looked so lovely, Esther thought, in her pale musliny frock, and with a little separate curl touching her cheek. And there was Andrew presiding—benign, fresh, large—clean white shirt-cuffs just showing below his sleeves. All was there to make perfect wholeness, roundness—a warm, golden bubble.

"I thought I should have died of heat in town to-day," said Ella.

"Then why did you go there, my dear?" boomed Andrew.

"Why, I had to. I was invited; I had to go out to lunch."

"Gadding about," said Andrew. "You're always gadding about. Can't you stay in your home occasionally?"

"Oh, but, Father, I do. You know I do. Why, I'm there at this moment, aren't I?"

"Yes, yes, yes, now. But still ..."

No, they had not spoilt it. All was well.

Back slid the chairs over the polished floor.

"Going upstairs," said Andrew. But he surveyed the table as if a little reluctant to leave it. He took a large, juicy-looking pear, felt it, was satisfied, and holding it went out of the room.

Frances moved tentatively to Esther's side. "We'll go out in the garden, shall we, dear?" said Esther. Then she looked across at Ella. Her eyes besought her.

"Are you going to come with us, Ella?"

"No. No, thanks," said Ella carelessly, and she looked away, "I'd rather not."

"Oh, yes, do, Ella dear!"

"No, no, I'd rather stay indoors."

But Esther so much wanted her to come. She wanted her to come so much that she couldn't help persisting.

"Yes, yes, Ella. I want you to. Do come. To please me."

"No!" cried Ella vehemently. "No, I tell you. I don't want to. To tell you the truth I—I'm utterly sick of your interference." Her voice rose. "Sick of it! I—I'm sick of you too. ... So there! What did you want to come here for, you—you—?"

"Oh," cried Frances, taking a long breath. Her nostrils expanded, all her little body stiffened up. "I think you're horrid, horrid, horrid! How *dare* you talk to my Miss King like that! She's the dearest, sweetest, bravest—"

"Pooh!" said Ella, and she tossed her head and laughed scornfully. "Bravest, indeed! What has *she* done, I should like to know?"

"Done?" cried Frances, looking about wildly for inspiration. "Why—why, don't you know that all the while at school—for four years—she was engaged to a dead person—to—to—"

"Oh, be quiet, Frances! Don't I tell you!" Esther grasped her firmly by the shoulder. Ella moved a hand as if to waive them both away.

"Oh, my dear little girl," she said calmly, "I don't believe it."

"Don't believe it!" cried Frances incredulously.

"No, no, of course I don't. They pretend they're engaged. She told you just to make you—"

"Ella!" Esther was furious now. Really she could hardly speak. "Out of my sight! Go on! Out of the room!" She pointed with a stiffened arm. "Either you go or I do. Out you go!"

Ella moved slowly across the room. But at the door she paused. She looked back. She smiled her maddening smile.

Then Frances turned to her mistress and flung her arms round her waist.

"Oh, dear, darling Miss King, don't, don't think about it! I'm here. I love you."

But Esther didn't respond. Oh, no. Instead she tried to shake her off.

"I don't want you, child. Leave me alone!" And because Frances still clung, she said, "No, no, *go,* I say!"

"Oh, Miss King!" wailed poor Frances.

But Esther took no notice. Quickly she pulled off Frances' hands. She flung the french window wide open.

And with her thoughts all in extraordinary chaos, she ran out into the dark garden.

My Mother

Jamaica Kincaid

Immediately on wishing my mother dead and seeing the pain it caused her, I was sorry and cried so many tears that all the earth around me was drenched. Standing before my mother, I begged her forgiveness, and I begged so earnestly that she took pity on me, kissing my face and placing my head on her bosom to rest. Placing her arms around me, she drew my head closer and closer to her bosom, until finally I suffocated. I lay on her bosom, breathless, for a time uncountable, until one day, for a reason she has kept to herself, she shook me out and stood me under a tree and I started to breathe again. I cast a sharp glance at her and said to myself, "So." Instantly I grew my own bosoms, small mounds at first, leaving a small, soft place between them, where, if ever necessary, I could rest my own head. Between my mother and me now were the tears I had cried, and I gathered up some stones and banked them in so that they formed a small pond. The water in the pond was thick and black and poisonous, so that only unnameable invertebrates could live in it. My mother and I now watched each other carefully, always making sure to shower the other with words and deeds of love and affection.

I was sitting on my mother's bed trying to get a good look at myself. It was a large bed and it stood in the middle of a large, completely dark room. The room was completely dark because all the windows had been boarded up and all the crevices stuffed with black cloth. My mother lit some candles and the room burst into a pink-like, yellow-like glow. Looming over us, much larger than ourselves, were our shadows. We sat mesmerised because our shadows had made a place between themselves, as if they were making room for someone else. Nothing filled up the space between them, and the shadow of my mother sighed. The shadow of my mother danced around the room to a tune that my own shadow sang, and then they stopped. All along, our shadows had grown thick and thin, long and short, had fallen at every angle, as if they were controlled by the light of day. Suddenly my mother got up and blew out the candles and our shadows vanished. I continued to sit on the bed, trying to get a good look at myself.

My mother removed her clothes and covered thoroughly her skin with a thick gold-coloured oil, which had recently been rendered in a hot pan from the livers of reptiles with pouched throats. She grew plates of metal-coloured scales on her back, and light, when it collided with this surface, would shatter and collapse into tiny points. Her teeth now arranged themselves into rows that reached all the way back to her long white throat. She uncoiled her hair from her head and then removed her hair altogether. Taking her head into her large palms, she flattened it so that her eyes, which were by now ablaze, sat on top of her head and spun like two revolving balls. Then, making two lines on the soles of each foot, she divided her feet into crossroads. Silently, she had instructed me to follow her example, and now I too travelled along on my white underbelly, my tongue darting and flickering in the hot air. "Look," said my mother.

My mother and I were standing on the seabed side by side, my arms laced loosely around her waist, my head resting securely on her shoulder, as if I needed the support. To make sure she believed in my frailness, I sighed occasionally—long soft sighs, the kind of sigh she had long ago taught me could evoke sympathy. In fact, how I really felt was invincible. I was no longer a child but I was not yet a woman. My skin had just blackened and cracked and fallen away and my new impregnable carapace had taken full hold. My nose had flattened; my hair curled in and stood out straight from my head simultaneously; my many rows of teeth in their retractable trays were in place. My mother and I wordlessly made an arrangement—I sent out my beautiful sighs, she received them; I leaned ever more heavily on her for support, she offered her shoulder, which shortly grew to the size of a thick plank. A long time passed, at the end of which I had hoped to see my mother permanently cemented to the seabed. My mother reached out to pass a hand over my head, a pacifying gesture, but I laughed and, with great agility, stepped aside. I let out a horrible roar, then a self-pitying whine. I had grown big, but my mother was bigger, and that would always be so. We walked to the Garden of Fruits and there ate to our hearts' satisfaction. We departed through the southwesterly gate, leaving as always, in our trail, small colonies of worms.

With my mother, I crossed, unwillingly, the valley. We saw a lamb grazing and when it heard our footsteps it paused and looked up at us. The lamb looked cross and miserable. I said to my mother, "The lamb is cross and miserable. So would I be, too, if I had to live in a climate not suited to my nature." My mother and I now entered the cave. It was the dark and cold cave. I felt something growing under my feet and I bent down to eat it. I stayed that way for years, bent over eating whatever I found growing under my feet. Eventually, I grew a special lens that would allow me to see in the darkest of darkness; eventually, I grew a special coat that kept me warm in the coldest of coldness. One day I saw my mother sitting on a rock. She said, "What a strange expression you have on your face. So cross, so miserable, as if you were living in a climate not suited to your nature." Laughing, she vanished. I dug a deep, deep hole. I built a beautiful house, a floorless house, over the deep, deep hole. I put in lattice windows, most favoured of windows by my mother, so perfect for looking out at people passing by without her being observed; I painted the house itself yellow, the windows green, colours I knew would please her. Standing just outside the door, I asked her to inspect the house. I said, "Take a look. Tell me if it's to your satisfaction." Laughing out of the corner of a mouth I could not see, she stepped inside. I stood just outside the door, listening carefully, hoping to hear her land with a thud at the bottom of the deep, deep hole. Instead, she walked up and down in every direction, even pounding her heel on the air. Coming outside to greet me, she said, "It is an excellent house. I would be honoured to live in it," and then vanished. I filled up the hole and burnt the house to the ground.

My mother has grown to an enormous height. I have grown to an enormous height also, but my mother's height is three times mine. Sometimes I cannot see from her breasts on up, so lost is she in the atmosphere. One day, seeing her sitting on the seashore, her hand reaching out in the deep to caress the belly of a striped fish as he swam through a place where two seas met, I glowed red with anger. For a while then I lived alone on the island where there were eight full moons and I adorned the face of each moon with expressions I had seen on my mother's face. All the expressions favoured me. I soon grew tired of living in this way and returned to my mother's side. I remained, though glowing red with anger, and my mother and I built houses on opposite banks of the dead pond. The dead pond lay between us; in it, only small invertebrates with poisonous lances lived. My mother behaved towards them as if she had suddenly found herself in the same room with relatives we had long since risen above. I cherished their presence and gave them names. Still I missed my mother's close company and cried constantly for her, but at the end of each day when I saw her return to her house, incredible and great deeds in her wake, each of them singing loudly her praises, I glowed and glowed again, red with anger. Eventually, I wore myself out and sank into a deep, deep sleep, the only dreamless sleep I have ever had.

One day my mother packed my things in a grip and, taking me by the hand, walked me to the jetty, placed me on board a boat, in care of the captain. My mother, while caressing my chin and cheeks, said some words of comfort to me because we had never been apart before. She kissed me on the forehead and turned and walked away. I cried so much my chest heaved up and down, my whole body shook at the sight of her back turned towards me, as if I had never seen her back turned towards me before. I started to make plans to get off the boat, but when I saw that the boat was encased in a large green bottle, as if it were about to decorate a mantelpiece, I fell asleep, until I reached my destination, the new island. When the boat stopped, I got off and I saw a woman with feet exactly like mine, especially around the arch of the instep. Even though the face was completely different from what I was used to, I recognised this woman as my mother. We greeted each other at first with great caution and politeness, but as we walked along, our steps became one, and as we talked, our voices became one voice, and we were in complete union in every other way. What peace came over me then, for I could not see where she left off and I began, or where I left off and she began.

My mother and I walk through the rooms of her house. Every crack in the floor holds a significant event: here, an apparently healthy young man suddenly dropped dead; here a young woman defied her father and, while riding her bicycle to the forbidden lovers' meeting place, fell down a precipice, remaining a cripple for the rest of a very long life. My mother and I find this a beautiful house. The rooms are large and empty, opening on to each other, waiting for people and things to fill them up. Our white muslin skirts billow up around our ankles, our hair hangs straight down our backs as our arms hang straight at our sides. I fit perfectly in the crook of my mother's arm, on the curve of her back, in the hollow of her stomach. We eat from the same bowl, drink from the same cup; when we sleep, our heads rest on the same pillow. As we walk through the rooms, we merge and separate, merge and separate; soon we shall enter the final stage of our evolution.

The fishermen are coming in from sea; their catch is bountiful, my mother has seen to that. As the waves plop, plop against each other, the fishermen are happy that the sea is calm. My mother points out the fishermen to me, their contentment is a source of my contentment. I am sitting in my mother's enormous lap. Sometimes I sit on a mat she has made for me from her hair. The lime trees are weighed down with limes—I have already perfumed myself with their blossoms. A hummingbird has nested on my stomach, a sign of my fertileness. My mother and I live in a bower made from flowers whose petals are imperishable. There is the silvery blue of the sea, crisscrossed with sharp darts of light, there is the warm rain falling on the clumps of castor bush, there is the small lamb bounding across the pasture, there is the soft ground welcoming the soles of my pink feet. It is in this way my mother and I have lived for a long time now.

Copyright Notices

'Week-End' by Richmal Crompton © Edward Ashbee and Catherine Massey.

'Maternal Devotion' by Sylvia Townsend Warner reproduced with kind permission of the author's estate.

'The Value of Being Seen' © Inez Holden reproduced with permission of the author's literary executor.

'Psalms' by Jeanette Winterson reprinted by permission of Peters, Fraser and Dunlop on behalf of Jeanette Winterson.

'The Pictures' by Janet Frame. Copyright © Janet Frame Estate, 2004, used by permission of The Wylie Agency (UK) Limited.

'Mothers and Daughters' by Frances Gray Patton reproduced with kind permission of the author's estate.

'The Shadow of Kindness' by Maeve Brennan. Reprinted by the permission of Russell & Volkening as agents for the author. Published in *The Springs of Affection* (Houghton Mifflin).

Copyright © 1998 by The Estate of Maeve Brennan. Copyright © 1969 by Maeve Brennan. Copyright © 1954, 1955, 1958, 1960, 1961, 1962, 1963, 1964, 1965, 1966, 1967, 1968 by *The New Yorker Magazine*, Inc. Copyright © 1955, 1962, 1967 by Maeve Brennan. Copyright © 1969, 1970, 1973, 1976, 1981 by *The New Yorker Magazine*, Inc.

'Rose-Coloured Teacups' © A. S. Byatt. Reproduced by kind permission of the estate and RCW Literary Agency.

'Love is Not a Pie' by Amy Bloom from *Come to Me: Short Stories* by Amy Bloom. Copyright © 1993 by Amy Bloom. Used by permission of HarperCollins Publishers and WME Agency.

'The Battle-Field' by Phyllis Bottome, from *Best Stories of Phyllis Bottome* Faber & Faber; reproduced by permission of David Higham Associates.

'I Stand Here Ironing' from *Tell Me a Riddle, Requa I, and Other Works* by Tillie Olsen. Copyright © 1961, 2013 by Tillie Olsen Estate. Reprinted by permission of The Frances Goldin Literary Agency and University of Nebraska Press.

'My Mother' by Jamaica Kincaid, From *At the Bottom of the River*, first published by Picador in 1984, Picador is an imprint of Pan Macmillan. Reproduced by permission of Macmillan Publishers International Limited and Farrar, Straus and Giroux. Copyright © Jamaica Kincaid 1978, 1979, 1981, 1982, 1983. All Rights Reserved.